PEACE & GOODWILL
THE MINSTREL SERIES

The Minstrel Series
Sun & Moon (#1)
Flesh & Bone (#2)
Heart & Soul (#3)
Peace & Goodwill (#4 ~ a Christmas novella)

LEE STRAUSS

THE MINSTREL SERIES

Peace & Goodwill
by Lee Strauss
Copyright © 2014 Lee Strauss

Cover by NovakIllustration.com
Formatting by NovelNinjutsu.com

ISBN: 9781927547304

This is a work of fiction and the views expressed herein are the sole responsibility of the author. Likewise, characters, places and incidents are either the product of the author's imagination or are represented fictitiously and any resemblance to actual persons, living or dead, or actual event or locales, is entirely coincidental.

All rights reserved.
This book, or parts thereof, may not be reproduced in any form without permission.

Belle gets the best Christmas present ever, a man in uniform! Ian is a soldier home on leave. Neither of them has any idea how good it will feel to fall in love or how hard it will be to say good-bye.

Anna is spending the holidays alone again with only her faithful dog, Angel, to keep her company. She can't afford to pay the rent, and her landlord threatens to kick her out. At least she's finished with her chemo treatments. She can be thankful for that. Plus, there's Rhys, the handsome visitor with kind eyes.

One fateful cold and snowy night, a chance encounter changes everything. Love is lost. Love is found. Life will never be the same.

Peace & Goodwill,
a Christmas novella in The Minstrel Series,
grabs the heartstrings and pulls hard.

Novels in the Minstrel Series:
Sun & Moon: Katja and Micah
Flesh & Bone: Eva and Sebastian
Heart & Soul: Gabriele and Callum

PERMISSIONS

THE CHRISTMAS SONG

Words and music by Andrew Smith. Copyright Andrew Smith. Remake recorded by Bethany Petch, produced by Norm Strauss. All rights reserved. Used by permission.

CONTENTS

A Time and a Season	…..	1
The Generosity of Strangers	…..	7
I'll Meet You	…..	12
The Great Escape	…..	17
Merry Christmas to Me	…..	22
Companion of the Loner	…..	28
The Millennium Wheel	…..	33
The Rose in the Briar	…..	44
Stupid, Stupid Girl	…..	47
The Kiss of the Lover	…..	54
Treasure of the Seeker	…..	56
Lying in Starlight	…..	66
Stay in the Moment	…..	70
Image of the Artist	…..	74
It's Christmastime	…..	77
New Year's Eve	…..	83
The Gift	…..	86
I've Missed You	…..	91
Time in Between Times	…..	94
Live Your Life	…..	97
Sample from East of the Sun	…..	
About the Author	…..	
Song Links	…..	
Artist Links	…..	
Acknowledgements	…..	
Books by Lee Strauss	…..	

A Time and a Season

Belle

Belle Vaughn swallowed the gluey lump that formed in her throat as she arranged the winter scene in the window of King's Used Book Shop. Mrs. Cowen could be very particular and she wanted the miniature replica of the popular landmarks of London and all its miniature inhabitants "to delight and entice" prospective shoppers into the shop.

Belle arranged the little carolers around the mini version of Saint Paul's Cathedral. Tiny trees and park benches dotted the edges of a curvy blue ribbon that represented the River Thames. Several small bridges along with the famed Tower Bridge. Miniature lampposts and streetcars, including the iconic red double-decker buses. She sprinkled shiny white confetti over everything for a snow-like touch, and plugged in the string of white lights she'd tacked around the window earlier that day.

She gasped at her creation, a beautiful, perfect little world. The pang in her heart deepened. A glance through the window reminded her that the real world wasn't so magical. She didn't live in the romantic ideal of central London, but in the lesser-visited east end, home of a significant immigrant population, along with the poor and working poor like herself.

Outside, holiday shoppers scampered, hunched over, chins buried into scarves, bodies pressed into the wind with no time or inclination to stop and gaze at the fanciful window display Belle had created. The real streets beyond the glass were dirty and the sky was a brooding grey. Nasty weather systems attacked the United Kingdom from the Arctic regions of the pacific.

Belle sighed and returned to the counter where a stack of books waited for her to catalogue, price and shelve.

"Any plans for Christmas this year, love?" Mrs. Cowen asked. She asked Belle this every year and every year Belle shook her head sheepishly. No. She was an orphan and without family. She'd lived alone in her little apartment for the last three years since her mother had passed away, and she didn't even have a pet because her miserable landlord forbade it.

"You're welcome to spend it with us," Mrs. Cowen said with a small smile. "Again."

Again. Mrs. Cowen was being polite. But the truth was Belle's presence at Mrs. Cowen's family Christmas was an intrusion. For the last two years she was the only non-family member sitting around the Cowen's dinner table. Everyone was always pleasant and polite—how could they not be? Belle was to be pitied. No parents, no family. It was their *duty* to include her. If the dinners were uncomfortable, her arrival to the Christmas morning gift opening was downright painful. After Mrs. Cowen's daughter and two granddaughters greeted her with fake smiles and stiff hugs, they basically pretended she wasn't in the room.

Being alone was preferable to being invisible.

Mrs. Cowen wore billowing blouses and skirts that hung loosely on a tall, thin frame. Her greying blond hair was permed in tight, short curls, and she penciled in her eyebrows, thin stark lines above sagging eyelids too tired to resist gravity any longer.

Belle put on her brave face and stared at her employer. "Thank you so much for the invitation, Mrs. Cowen, but I've accepted another this year." It was a lie, but by the expression of relief that flickered briefly across Mrs. Cowen's face, Belle knew she did the right thing.

"That's fantastic," Mrs. Cowen said. "I'm so glad you're making friends." *Finally*. She didn't say it, but it was implied. *Finally*, she was recovering from her mother's long drawn out illness and death. *Finally* she was making friends her own age (presumably), finally, she was *moving on*.

If only it were true. Belle sighed and physically shook her shoulders in an effort to break free from the gloom that plagued her. Christmas was supposed to be the happiest time of the year, but for her the opposite was true.

She donned her reading glasses and got to work. Nothing like losing oneself in a mass of accounting numbers to forget ones problems.

The bell tinkled above the door and a blast of cold air

came in with a customer. Belle glanced up over her glasses. Standing inside the shop was a man, about her age, mid-twenties or so, dressed in army fatigues. He removed his hat when he saw her. She slipped off her glasses.

Air escaped her lungs and her jaw went slack. He was very good looking—what girl didn't love a man in a uniform? His hair was buzzed short, blond with a hint of red, his face shaved clean, and he had a firm jaw and straight nose. His skin was ruddy with a smattering of freckles. His eyes were dark in the light of the shop and they crinkled at the corners when he smiled. At her. Belle's heart flittered around like a bird wanting out of a cage. She pushed her short, dark hair behind her ears in a nervous response.

"Can I help you?" she squeaked out.

The soldier ducked his chin as he shook his head. "Just looking."

Belle was grateful she didn't have to stand or walk about the shop for the soldier because quite honestly, she didn't trust her knees at this point. Her joints felt like pools of water.

She put her glasses back on and pretended to busy herself, but who was she kidding? How could she concentrate on bookwork with a guy like *him* in the shop? Her eyes darted repeatedly to the soldier, careful that he didn't catch her staring.

Until he did. He glanced from the book in his hand to where she sat behind the counter and then away again. They played that game for several minutes until a chuckle escaped her lips and she slapped a hand over her mouth.

It appeared the soldier had selected a book and approached her. Belle removed her glasses and wiped damp palms on her black trousers.

He slid a gently used version of Stephen Lawhead's book *The Paradise War*, first book in the *Song of Albion Trilogy*, across the counter.

"Nice choice," she said.

"Thanks." The soldier stared at her name tag, then added, "Belle Vaughn."

Belle rang up his order, and the soldier handed her a five-pound note. "I'm Lieutenant Ian Connor, by the way. Since I know your name, I thought it only fair to tell you mine."

"I appreciate the equal opportunity," Belle said with a grin. She motioned to his uniform "Are you recently back or on your way out?"

"I'm on leave for a month."

"Nice for you to be home for Christmas." She slipped his purchase into a bag and handed it to him.

Ian smiled. "It sure is." He tucked the bag under his arm. "Thanks."

Just as he grabbed the doorknob, Belle blurted, "Thanks for shopping at King's Books. We hope to see you again!"

Oh, God. Her face burned with embarrassment. Why did she feel compelled to yell out that dumb, rote response? Mrs. Cowen had drilled it into her, but there was a time and a season for everything (a quote from her mother, God rest her soul), and this was not the time or season for *that*.

Ian's eyes narrowed quizzically. "I hope so, too."

Belle wiggled her fingers. "Bye, Lieutenant Connor."

The soldier disappeared out the door, and Belle slumped into her chair with a groan. No wonder she was still single.

THE GENEROSITY OF STRANGERS

Anna

Anna pulled her winter jacket closed over her chest as she padded across her cramped flat in worn-out slippers. A tug on the fridge handle just confirmed what she already knew. Except for a near-empty container of orange juice and a quarter block of butter it was empty.

A cold nose nudged her arm and she reached down to scrub the ears of her collie. "Mornin' Angel." Anna filled her bowl, frowning at the almost-empty bag of dog food.

She poured the juice into a glass and tossed the empty carton into the trash. The citrus burned her throat but she chugged it down anyway. She didn't feel hungry but dropped two pieces of bread in the toaster and buttered them when they popped.

She stared out the window as she ate, fighting against the constant shivering that wracked her body. Even though there was a break in the cold weather she couldn't get warm. It didn't help that Mr. Hutchens, her landlord, had cut the heat. Cranky old coot.

Anna frowned. She couldn't pay the rent again and all Mr. Hutchens had to say about that was that she better not die before squaring up.

She had thirty days to either kick off or pay up and since the doctors couldn't say for sure how long she had left, she better try to scrounge up some rent. Anna put on an extra layer of clothes and tightened the thin, cotton-blend scarf on her bald head before adding a wool cap. Her temples throbbed under her fingertips, and a painful bolt seared her head causing her to yelp. She reached for her pills and quickly swallowed one, chasing it with a glass of tepid water.

If there was one good thing about Christmas, it was that it put people in the mood for giving.

"Come, girl," Anna commanded and was rewarded by a wagging tail and a lick on the hand. She snapped the leash to the collar then clasped the handle of her guitar case. Her upper-floor flat exited out onto several sets of weather-worn, open-slat stairs to a narrow lane below. It was getting tougher to manage in her weakened physical state and she gripped the tarnished iron rail tightly. She was glad it hadn't started snowing yet. Mr. Hutchens told his tenants they needed to do the shoveling themselves. Anna sighed and continued down, unsure how she would manage that task when the time came.

She couldn't afford to hire help. All she could do was pray that it wouldn't snow.

Anna rounded the bend of the first flight of stairs ignoring the litter that had piled up in the corner. Angel looked up at her with wide, brown eyes, her tongue wagging as if she was cheering on Anna. The dog never tugged on the leash, always descending at the pace Anna dictated. She paused at the bottom to catch her breath and then made her way to the street with her dog and guitar in hand, the only two things of value that she owned.

She walked past the bus stop just as a red double-decker stopped for a Nigerian family dressed in colorful jackets to board, and then she ventured down along the shopping district of Station Parade.

Angel barked as Anna hurried past the used book store. She frowned and tugged gently on her pet's leash. "Shh, girl." Anna's eyes darted to the window—at the tired-looking mini-London display—for just a moment until she pulled her gaze to the train station ahead.

Anna chose a spot near the entrance, around the corner from a small WH Smith bookstore that faced the ticket counter. The slight rise in temperatures had brought the shoppers out in hoards, many heading into London via the tube so that they walked right by the spot where Anna positioned herself to play. She removed her guitar, leaving her case open, hoping for the generosity of strangers.

"Angel sit," she said, and the animal's hind end promptly lowered to the ground. Anna stood near the brick wall. She closed her eyes, breathed in as deeply as possible and then played her favorite Christmas carol.

Silent Night, Holy Night
All is calm, all is bright

Despite the rush brought on by the holiday season, passersby stopped to listen. Anna's voice remained strong and clear, contrary to what her physique suggested. The words of the carol were very familiar to her, but today, as she closed her eyes and sang toward heaven like she had nothing to lose, she felt overwhelmed. A lone tear streamed down her face unbidden. She didn't have much to show for this life, but she'd loved and had been loved, and that was all she could ask for.

"So beautiful," a voice said, breaking her reverie. Anna opened her eyes to see a man smiling kindly at her. He was middle-aged with short dark hair greying at the temples. His eyes were a warm hazel and they crinkled at the corners.

She smiled back and wiped at her face, hoping the handsome stranger hadn't noticed her emotion. "Thank you."

"I'd like to buy a CD."

Anna's eyes widened in surprise. She had a small stack sitting in her guitar case, but it'd been ages since anyone had bought one, at least since the summer. She motioned to the case and named the price. "Help yourself."

The man picked one up and examined the cover. There was a photo of her on the back from before she'd lost her hair. It had been long and brown and she used to have dark eyebrows. Now she had neither. The man's eyes flickered from the picture to her new hairless look and back to the picture. He dropped twice the amount she'd asked for into her case.

"That's too much," she said. "Why don't you take two?"

"You don't have that many left. I don't want to rob others of the pleasure." He knelt down in front of Angel.

"Nice dog. He or she?"

"She."

"Can I pet her?"

"Of course."

He scrubbed Angel's ears and she panted happily in response. "You're a nice girl, now, aren't you?"

Anna couldn't help but smile at the two of them.

The man stretched back into a standing position and stepped away. "I won't keep you any longer." He offered a lazy salute. "Merry Christmas, miss."

"Merry Christmas to you." Anna blew on her red fingers and started playing again.

Belle

With only one bay window facing the street and flanked by a variety of shops on either side, Kings Used Book Shop wasn't a large store. It ran about three times as deep as it was wide and rows of old wooden bookshelves took up most of the floor space. Belle hung Christmas decorations from the ceiling and along the counter to give the space a holiday feel, but most people came for the nostalgia found in the pages. Many books were older than the patrons themselves.

A young woman entered holding the hand of a preschooler. A bluster of cold air followed them in.

"Can I help you?" Belle asked.

"I hope so," the woman replied. "My mother-in-law is a Jane Austen fan and I'm hoping to find a special edition of one of her classics as a Christmas gift."

"Ah, Jane Austen is a favorite, and happily we have many editions to choose from." Belle led the woman and her daughter to the appropriate shelf. She pulled out an early edition of *Persuasion*. "This came in recently. Still in very good condition."

"Thank you." The woman flipped through the pages and examined the spine. "I'll consider it."

Belle wiggled her fingers at the little girl and smiled wistfully. She wondered, would she ever know the joy of motherhood? She muffled a groan. Not at this rate. She was destined to be one of those cat ladies, except her landlord wouldn't let her have a cat, so she'd just be alone with an ancient telly to keep her company.

Her mind flickered back to the soldier from the day before: Lieutenant Ian Connor. She couldn't keep the handsome man from her daydreams which only underlined how pathetic she was. She rested her chin in her palm and closed her eyes. Yes, in her dreams the soldier returned to the shop, swept her off her feet and whisked her away to somewhere warm and exotic, freeing her from the solitude and drudgery her life had become. They'd walk hand in hand among frothy, lapping waves, and eventually, when the sun burned orange on the horizon, they'd collapse onto the sandy beach, their bare legs twisting together. He'd snog her passionately like lovers do (she wouldn't know from personal experience, but she *had* read a lot of romance novels) and profess his undying love.

She'd whisper his name urgently in his ear, *Ian*.

"Belle?"

Belle's eyes snapped open and she shrieked. Lieutenant Ian Connor stood on the other side of the counter, eyes narrowed in concern.

Oh, God, had she said his name aloud? She was so absorbed in her daydream, she hadn't even heard the bell ring.

"Are you all right?" Ian said. "I hope I didn't startle you."

"No, yes. I mean, yes, I'm all right. And well, yes, you did startle me." She faked a yawn and patted her mouth. "I really must get a better rest tonight."

"Trouble sleeping?" he asked.

The truth was she did have trouble sleeping most nights, but last night she'd dreamt of him, and yes, there had been snogging. She felt her face burn.

"I know what it's like to struggle with insomnia," Ian continued. "Hot milk really does work."

"I'll try that," Belle said, bobbing her head. "Tonight."

Ian held his army cap in his hands and stared at Belle as if at a loss for words.

"How was *The Paradise War*?" Belle asked. "Have you finished it already?"

"Not finished, but I can tell I'll want the next book right away when I do." He smiled then, and Belle's heart jumped and skipped and scampered about. "Do you mind directing me to the proper shelves?" he added. "They all look the same to me."

"Certainly." Belle moved from behind the counter and Ian followed closely. The air between them felt charged with electricity. Was it her imagination? It had been going pretty wild lately, especially where Lieutenant Connor was concerned.

She grabbed at her heart and breathed deeply. The comfortable, musky scent of old books always had a calming effect on her nerves and she counted on that to help her now.

"This is the fantasy section," Belle managed. "And this is where the authors with last names starting with *L* are." She bent down to tug on the second volume and pinched her eyes together. *He was standing so close to her.* The buttons of his jacket brushed against her back as she stood. She turned and he didn't step back. To be fair, the aisles *were* narrow, but he could've sidestepped.

"This is it," she mustered.

"Will you have dinner with me?"

Belle's breath hitched and something—saliva? dust?—went down the wrong way. Her chest heaved as she engaged in a most ungraceful bout of coughing. She covered her mouth and twisted to the side.

Ian patted her on the back. "Belle?"

"I'm fine," she choked out. "Just…" She covered her face. Her eyes watered and were likely a bloodshot mess, not to mention her matching unattractively blotchy face. She took quick steps back to the counter wishing she could curl up underneath it and die.

Ian followed her. "I'm going to assume that you're not looking for an excuse to say no to me. Am I right?"

Belle covered her face and nodded. She was such an *idiot*.

"Great!" Ian said. "Can I pick you up at eight?"

Belle pictured him coming to her run-down flat and blanched. Managing to compose herself she dared to look at his eyes. His expression was hopeful and she was shocked he still wanted to take her out after such an unflattering bronchial demonstration.

She heard herself say, "I'll meet you."

He looked relieved, like he really thought there was a possibility she would backtrack and say no. (Not a chance.)

"Okay." He named a popular Indian restaurant, then pushed the book in his hand across the counter. "Hold this for me." He winked as he stepped backwards to the door. "So I have an excuse to come back again."

THE GREAT ESCAPE

Anna

A wave of nausea and dizziness forced Anna to lean against the wall and slink to the cement floor. She closed her eyes and waited for the wooziness to pass, gripping the arm of her guitar with cold fingers. The episodes were lasting longer each time, and Anna didn't know if she could continue to take to the cold outdoors and play for money. Certainly no more today. She mopped the beads of cold sweat from her brow with her wool glove and then studied the contents of her guitar case. Besides the one twenty-pound note given to her by that kind gentleman, the rest of her earnings were in the form of coins. She removed a glove to collect them and deposited them in her pocket.

"Time to go, ol' girl." The collie wagged a tail and fell obediently into step by her side. Anna trod carefully. No sense falling and creating a scene. Anna preferred when people averted their eyes. It was easier than having to deal with the pity she saw there. Thankfully, Angel distracted onlookers from prolonged observations of Anna's drawn face or hairless head and missing eyebrows. Anna rattled the coins in her pocket as she approached a small market. She hated those big grocery stores with bright lights that bothered her eyes and made her thin skin look almost translucent. She disliked how everyone there pushed large carts and were always in a hurry.

No, she preferred the calmer, warmer atmosphere of a family run store like the one manned by Asian immigrants. She didn't mind that their English wasn't perfect. It meant they were less likely to try to engage in conversation. Anna never felt like talking.

She tied Angel up to a bike rack and patted her head. "I'll be right back." If the weather were better, she'd take her guitar and Angel home first and come back to shop later, but the thought of making a second trip made her bones heavy with weariness. Better to just do it now and get it over with, even if it meant lugging her heavy guitar around.

Anna collected a basket and tossed in a few basics: bread, cheese—no meat, it turned her stomach—a couple bananas, a tomato, and a small bag of dog food. She stood in the queue and was stunned by the appearance of the man who bought her CD as he joined the line behind her. She looked away quickly feeling shy. It was one thing to be a performer and talk to people about music and an entirely other thing to make small talk with a stranger in a random shop. She lay her guitar down on the ground and her items on the counter, hoping the man wouldn't recognize her. Her guitar was a giveaway.

"Hi there!"

Anna blinked. She heard his voice and he knew it, so she couldn't very well ignore him. She glanced at him and forced a smile. It was kind of him to go out of his way to speak to her, but she wished he wasn't quite so good-looking. She subconsciously swiped fingers over her ear, forgetting that she hadn't any hair to push behind it.

She swallowed and forced herself to respond. "Hello."

Thankfully, he didn't continue to speak to her. She quickly paid for her things and headed back out into the wintery weather.

"Oh, you poor thing." Anna bent down to release Angel's leash from the bike stand. "We'll be home soon." She tucked her chin in her scarf and trudged forward. She paused briefly when they passed the used books store again. Christmas music pumped out of small speakers above the window. An embossed, metal sign on the door needed painting: *Find the Great Escape in Books.*

The pang in Anna's chest charged the rest of her body. She sighed, stared straight ahead and continued walking.

"Hey, Anna!"

No one ever called after her. Anna knew who it was before she turned to face him. He jogged after her, his smile spread wide on his face.

"Can I carry your guitar for you? Your arms look full with your groceries, and having to lead your dog as well."

Anna's mouth opened but no sound came out.

"I'm Rhys, by the way." He held out his hand. "Rhys Williams."

Anna slowly lowered her guitar to the ground and extended her arm to shake the man's hand. "How do you do?"

Rhys picked up her guitar and it did, in fact, ease her load. The instrument was heavy and her arm burned from the weight of it.

Anna had noticed the high quality of Rhys's overcoat and his expensive boots. She was certain he didn't call the east end of London home. "What brings you to Barking?" she asked.

"Family. In-laws, actually. My wife passed away two years ago. We were married for twenty-one years. I got on well with her family, and so I still come to visit once in a while."

"I'm sorry to hear about your wife."

He just nodded and stared at the slushy ground beneath their feet. Anna wondered if she should be concerned about showing a virtual stranger where she lived, even though she appreciated the help. Ironically, the presence of her landlord comforted her should Mr. Williams not turn out to be the gentleman she believed him to be. Mr. Hutchen and his wife lived in the flat beneath her, right above the cupcake shop and the neighbouring hair salon. Their arguments along with the conflicting scents of sweet cakes and nostril-burning chemicals often wafted up to her flat.

They passed the bus stop and entered the alley between the shops that opened to a series of staircases that led to the above-shop flats.

"This is where I live."

Anna watched for a flicker of judgment to flash across Rhys's face but his expression didn't change. She unleashed Angel before trudging up the stairs. The dog sprung ahead, slowing as she neared the top. Rhys followed behind her with her guitar.

She worked the key into the lock and opened the door. Without stepping in behind her, Rhys leaned over and set her guitar down inside.

"Thank you," she said.

"My pleasure." Rhys smiled again. "I'm pleased to have made your acquaintance. I look forward to going back to my in-laws' and playing your CD. Once again, I wish you a Happy Christmas."

"And I to you."

Anna stared at the back of the door as Rhys closed it behind him. Rhys Williams was a pleasant man and meeting him had brought a ray of sunshine to her day.

Anna settled in on her sofa and Angel curled up by her legs.

"That was an unexpected turn, wasn't it girl? If only our situation were different."

If only.

However, Anna wasn't getting any healthier and her dog wasn't getting any younger. She petted the top of Angel's silky head. What was going to happen to her pet when she died? Anna knew she needed to make arrangements soon, but she just hadn't had the heart to face it yet. Tears welled up behind her eyes at the thought of saying good-bye to her only real friend. She'd make some inquiries in the morning.

Belle

A date! She was going on an actual date. Belle never expected presents at Christmas time, but this was more than she could've hoped for. Dinner with Lieutenant Ian Connor. *Merry Christmas to me.*

If only she had something nice to wear. Belle let out a frustrated sigh. The best she could do was an off-white jumper with a pair of clean jeans. She showered, squealing when the water fluxed from hot to cold, and quickly washed her short brown hair. She used to wear it long, but she'd chopped it off, barely able to see what she was doing through her angry tears the night her mother died. It was her way of grieving, and Belle had left her pile of hair wherever it had fallen, in the sink and on the floor, for a whole week before she finally swept it up and tossed it in the rubbish bin.

Now she kept her hair in a bob just past her chin and scooped the loose strands behind her ears. Belle's mum had left her a small collection of jewelry, nothing of real value, just costume, and Belle chose a pair of silver hoop earrings. Belle never left her flat without at least a little makeup on, especially mascara. She added a second coat for the occasion, hoping it brightened her pale green eyes, and added a layer of pink gloss to her lips.

She stood back to examine her image. Was she pretty? Not really. Not in a conventional way. Her nose was a little too big and her breasts a little too small. But she had nice eyes, strong cheekbones and a slender figure, so that helped to make up for what she lacked.

Ian seemed to like what he saw, and that was what mattered in the end.

Belle wished she had a nicer winter jacket, but she had picked up a new silky jade green scarf recently because her mother always told her the color brought out the green in her eyes, and that would be the thing people noticed.

She glanced at her watch. Should she be there when he arrived or should she keep him waiting a little? She locked the door of her flat on her way out. She wanted to show up at the restaurant right on time.

Ian was waiting for her in the entrance when she arrived. She smiled as she thought of him so eager for their date that he'd gotten there early. The waitress led them to a booth and Belle slid into the bench seat across from him. He wore his uniform again.

"Do you always have to wear that?"

He glanced down and back again. "You don't like it?"

"Yes, of course I do. You look very…" She looked away suddenly feeling shy.

"I look…dashing?" Ian prodded with a glint in his eye.

She giggled. "Yes, you look dashing. I just meant, do you get bored wearing it all the time?"

"Yes and no. I can wear civilian clothes if I want to, but I like how people treat me when I'm in uniform."

"How's that?"

"With respect. When I'm in normal clothes, I'm just another young punk."

"Well, you look very unpunkish to me."

"And you look smashing to me."

Belle's eyes grew wide and her heart fluttered at his praise. Thankfully, the waitress arrived with menus before she had to come up with a response.

Belle stared hard at the menu. She hadn't eaten out in a long time and really didn't know what all the Indian dishes were. She made barely enough working at the bookstore to cover her rent, utilities and basic needs. She certainly didn't have extra to spend at restaurants. Was she supposed to pay for herself? She gulped. And if not, she didn't want Ian to splurge on her.

Ian tapped her menu, startling her. "It's my treat remember," he said as if he could read her mind. "Order whatever you want."

"That's the thing. I don't know what I want."

"Would you like me to order for you?"

Belle nodded. "That'd be great. And there's nothing I don't like, so I'm fine with whatever you have."

It was obvious to Belle that Ian had eaten at Indian restaurants before since he knew exactly what he wanted and ordered five different dishes and an extra bowl of rice. She tried to keep the surprise off her face, but then again, he was a *soldier* and *strong* and probably ate way more than she did on a regular basis.

"So, tell me about yourself," Ian said.

"What do you want to know?"

"How long have you worked at Kings Books?"

"Three years."

"You must like it."

"I do. I love books and I love to read. Mrs. Cowen lets me read anything I want as long as I'm very gentle with the books, which I am. It's a great perk."

"Do you have family?"

Belle's heart dropped. She hated this question. "No, not really," she answered quietly. "I'm an only child, never knew my father, and my mother passed away two years ago of breast cancer." There, all her sadness out at once.

She dared to look up at him under her lashes, nervous that he'd be uncomfortable with her downer story. She waited for him to quickly change the subject to something lighter.

"My parents are gone, too," he said gently. He reached across the table and cupped Belle's hand with his. "We're both orphans."

Belle held her breath. Her nerves shot off as she took in the warmth of Ian's skin on hers, his rough, calloused palm on her soft, unblemished hand. She couldn't help but quiver.

Ian squeezed lightly and pulled his hand away. "I live with my gran when I'm here. I also have a sister but I hardly see her. She married an oil baron and lives in Saudi Arabia."

"How long have you been enlisted?" Belle asked.

"Three years. My father was an army man and it seemed natural for me to follow in his footsteps."

"Is that how he died?" she ventured.

Ian nodded. "In service of the Queen."

The server arrived with a tray full of ravishingly delicious-smelling meals. Belle's stomach growled. She was used to being in a constant state of near hunger and her senses went wild.

Afterwards, she allowed Ian to walk her home. He'd given her no reason to be afraid of him and in fact his presence brought her a sense of security. She was more concerned about a potential first kiss. Did he expect one on the first date? Did she? She glanced quickly at his lips Her cheeks grew warm.

What was she thinking? She didn't know if there'd even be a second date. She was getting way ahead of herself.

"I had a really nice time," she said as they stood face to face on the pavement behind her building. "Thank you."

"I had a nice time, too, Belle. I... fancy you."

A bubbly thrill coursed its way from the tips of her toes. "I fancy you, too."

He smiled so widely, his eyes nearly disappeared. "Good. I'll be by the store tomorrow to get that book."

"Right," she said. "You better get home and finish reading the first one."

"I better." He leaned in and for a split second, Belle thought he would kiss her. She hadn't kissed a lad since... well, years, and that awkward experience had been nothing to write home about. Her heart pounded. She stiffened just a little.

Ian's lips moved to the side of her face and gently brushed against her cheek. It was tender and lovely and almost more than Belle's heart could take, so it was a good thing he hadn't tried a full on-snog.

"G'night," Ian whispered in her ear.

"G'night."

Belle waited until Ian disappeared around the corner then did a little jig and giggled quietly all the way up the slippery stairs to her flat.

COMPANION OF THE LONER

Anna

"Lie very still."

Anna kept her arms stiff along the length of her torso, damp palms pressed against her thighs. She could keep her body still, but she had no control over the rapid beating of her heart. She hated small spaces. Every time she had a CAT scan, it was the same thing: heart palpitations, cold beads of sweat sprouting on her bald, bare head, gravity pulling slow rivulets down her temples until they pooled in her ears.

She pinched her eyes tight and imagined a wide-open plain, warm wind sweeping across grassy fields, rolling hills carpeted in lavender, a sunrise bruising the horizon. Anything except the choking weight of claustrophobia.

Breathe in. Out.

And then it was over. A nurse smiled at her kindly and handed her a towel. Anna ran it over her face and head and accepted the plastic cup of water the nurse gave her in exchange for the soiled towel.

Anna was left alone in an examination room to get dressed. The hospital gown dropped to the cool floor and she slipped easily into her jeans and jumper. All her clothes hung loosely on her boney frame now. She wrapped the scarf on her head and stared at the stranger in the mirror. She barely recognized herself. Without eyebrows and lashes her eyes seemed to disappear: however, her nose and cheekbones were more pronounced and skeletal—a caricature of her former self. Anna sighed and fished through her purse for a powder compact. She lightly dusted her face to even out the tone. She followed that with eyeliner, which helped a little to create the illusion that she still had eyes, and applied lip balm to her lips.

Anna didn't know why she bothered. There was no one to impress, no one who cared if she was ugly or not. She was only fooling herself anyway. Makeup didn't change anything. It didn't make her beautiful. It didn't hide that she was sick.

At the same time, it was the one thing she could control. And deep down she knew the moment she stopped trying, she'd have given up. And when she gave up, she'd die.

She wasn't ready to die yet.

A tap on the door indicated the doctor was on the other side.

"Come in," Anna said.

The doctor sat on the edge of a stool, pushed wire-framed glasses up on his nose and studied the clipboard in his hand. "I'm afraid it's not good news."

Anna's insides squeezed together tight yet felt like jelly. She wrapped her arms around her chest and lifted her chin. "I didn't think it would be."

"Despite your chemo treatments and radiation, the tumor has grown. Have your headaches worsened?"

Anna nodded and rubbed her left temple.

The doctor nodded. "The tumor has grown. I'm not surprised you're feeling more pressure." He took a prescription pad out of his pocket, scribbled on it, ripped off the top sheet and handed it to her. "This should help with pain management. It's stronger than what you've been taking so far."

"Any side effects?" Anna asked. Her stomach turned at the memory of her many vomiting sessions. The good thing was she'd never have to do chemo again. The bad thing was she'd gone through three sessions, and she was still going to die.

"Drowsiness. You'll want to sleep a lot, and that's something I recommend you do anyway." The doctor paused at the door before leaving. "If things get bad, call 999 and get to the hospital."

If things get bad. Anna knew he meant *when*.

"Thank you," was all she said.

She bundled up with a wool cap, scarf, gloves and winter coat. With no body fat to speak of she needed all the help she could get to brace against the damp cold of winter.

She picked up her prescription using the last bit of cash left in her wallet and wondered what she'd do for food. She could visit the soup kitchen at the shelter again, she supposed.

At least she had that. Yes, thank God for the good people who offered help to the homeless this time of year.

With nowhere to go in a hurry, Anna found herself drawn to the church bells of St. Margaret's Church. She stopped to look at the nativity scene lit up with lights. A light snow danced in the lamplight and Anna couldn't help but admire the beauty and inhale the serenity. She decided she'd attend on Sunday.

The weekend hurried by in a blur of drowsiness. The doctor had been right about her new meds making her sleepy. She barely had the energy to feed and walk her dog. When Sunday morning came along, she forced herself to get dressed for church. If she was going to go to the trouble of trying to extend her life, she had to at least try to live it a little.

Anna was quite exhausted when she finally arrived at the ancient, stone abbey. She was late and the service was half over. She debated whether or not she should go in. The door of the church opened and a man in a trench coat stepped out and lit a cigarette. It would be warm inside, and that was incentive enough. She walked past the man who nodded slightly before a puff of smoke escaped through his nostrils.

Heavy, well-oiled wooden doors opened to the back of a long and narrow, white-washed sanctuary. Two rows of wooden pews dotted with parishioners ran from back to front. Anna slipped into an empty row at the very back.

The minister, who stood on a podium on a small elevated area, was clearly in the middle of his Christmas message.

"And lo, the angel of the Lord came upon them, and the glory of the Lord shone 'round about them, and they were afraid.

"And the angel said to them, 'Fear not, for behold, I bring you good tidings of great joy, which shall be to all people.'"

Hot tears pricked the back of Anna's eyes. *Fear not?* How could she not be afraid? She was alone and death was a black, shrouded stalker waiting to take her. The truth was she was afraid. She was terrified.

THE MILLENNIUM WHEEL

Belle

Belle hummed as she dusted the shelves, enjoying the mindlessness of the task since it allowed her thoughts to roam free. She felt like Cinderella in the fairytale after meeting the prince. The way Ian stared at her, his eyes crinkling with amusement and curiosity, and… longing—she felt like a princess, like he saw her dressed in a gown with a tiara instead of the cleaning rags she really wore.

"Aren't we in a good mood," Mrs. Cowen noted. Her penciled-on eyebrow arched. "Is it possible you've met a boy?"

Belle couldn't stop the flush that crept up her neck. Her body was so disloyal!

"Ah, there is a boy," Mrs. Cowen said with a smirk. "It's about time. Aren't you going to tell me about 'im?"

Belle was actually dying to tell someone. Had she met Ian three years ago, she'd have told her friends Marta and Beth all about him. When Belle's mother's health worsened, Belle dropped everything except for work and caring for her mother. She didn't have time for her friends then, and they didn't have time for her now.

"He's a new customer," she said. "We got to talking, and he asked me to dinner."

"Ooh," Mrs. Cowen cooed. "Love at first sight!"

Love? Was it love? "No, Mrs. Cowen, it was just a date."

"A date that made Belle Vaughn sing."

Belle rolled her eyes and wondered how on earth she was going to escape Mrs. Cowen's poking around in her personal business. The phone rang and Mrs. Cowen hurried to answer it. Belle returned to her dusting, thinking she'd been spared.

"Belle," Mrs. Cowen sang out. "It's for yo-ou."

Belle almost dropped her duster. No one rang for her. Ever.

Mrs. Cowen held a palm over the receiver as she handed it to Belle with a grin. "It's your fella."

Belle's nerves sent flares into the ceiling. "Hello?"

"Hi, Belle, it's Ian. I hope it's okay I rang you at the shop. I forgot to ask you for your number last night."

"No, it's fine." She didn't bother telling him she couldn't afford a phone of her own anyway.

"I couldn't stop thinking about you last night."

Belle's throat instantly dried up at his words. *He thought about her.* The same way she'd been thinking about him. "Me, too."

"Can I see you again?"

Belle's eyes flickered to Mrs. Cowen who studied her with interest. Her boss was enjoying this too much. She must miss the soaps she watched when she didn't come into work, and this was as close as she could get in real life. Belle turned her shoulder to the woman and kept her voice low. "Yes. I'd like that."

"Great! Unfortunately, I'm tied up tonight, but are you free tomorrow?"

"Yes, I am. It's my day off."

"Brilliant. Is it okay if I pick you up at your place?"

She wasn't ready for him to see her flat. She'd been forced to sell off some of their furniture to pay bills, and she was embarrassed at its sparseness. Besides, she didn't really know Ian that well, and she'd promised her mother she'd be careful when it came to boys. "I'll meet you on my steps." Her flat was among many, and if she were ever in trouble, all she had to do was yell, and one of her nosy neighbors would pop their head out of a window.

Ian agreed to meet her at two in the afternoon the next day. Belle handed the phone back to Mrs. Cowen. Try as she might, Belle couldn't stop a huge smile from commandeering her face.

"Another date, eh?" Mrs. Cowen's eyebrows danced. "Where's he taking you?"

"He wouldn't say. It's a surprise."

Mrs. Cowen clapped her hands. "Oh, I can't wait to hear all about it."

Belle turned away before rolling her eyes, even though it made her glad to have someone to share her happy news with.

Belle spent the next day and a half in a soupy, emotional fog. She fancied a boy! He fancied her.

She was gobsmacked that she'd garnered the attention of someone so extremely dishy. Goodness, those eyes! Golden brown, the colour of a penny. And how they almost disappeared when he smiled? Just so adorable.

Belle opened the doors of her wardrobe and frowned. If only she had something nicer to wear. She donned her prettiest sweater and nicest jeans. She pinned back her fringe with two silver barrettes and pushed her short hair behind her ears to reveal silver stud earrings. A little mascara and lip gloss and she was ready to go. She checked the time. Five minutes to two. She quickly pulled on her jacket and scarf, but carried her hat. She didn't want to mess her hair before he had a chance to see her put together.

Ian was already standing at the bottom of her steps when she opened the building's exterior door. Gosh, he was an early bird.

His face broke into a smile, stirring up the butterflies that had nested in her stomach since the day they'd met. She smiled back as she descended, careful to keep a hand on the rail so she wouldn't slip on the light dusting of snow. "Hi."

"Hi," he answered back. "You look nice."

She giggled. "Thanks. So do you."

Ian wore civilian clothes, the first time she'd seen him in jeans, and Belle swooned a little more.

"So, where are we going?" she asked.

"Have you ever been on the Millennium Wheel?"

Belle gasped. Many times, when she just needed to get away, she'd hop on the District Line to downtown London to see the sights and watch the people. She'd watched that monstrous Ferris wheel as it was being built, but had never ridden on it. "It's so high."

"Four hundred and forty-three feet tall, to be exact. Have you been on?" he asked again.

She shook her head.

"I went on it in 2000 just after it opened. You can see the whole city. It's fabulous. You'll love it."

Belle had been watching people ride the London Eye, as it was also known, since it opened. She'd never gone on it because she'd been too preoccupied with her mother's ill health during most of those years, and it seemed a frivolous waste of money.

She also didn't like heights. Just looking up to the top of the massive machine made her stomach slide.

"It's really high," she repeated.

Ian laughed. "You definitely need to ride it."

He reached for her hand, and she wished she hadn't just put on her gloves. Still, it felt nice that he was holding onto her that way and she decided she didn't care if she was catapulted into space or not. She was just going to enjoy being with him.

They rode the district line tube, chatting casually about nothing. Sitting across the narrow aisle was an Indian woman dressed in a bright orange sari with a small child sleeping across her lap. Beside her were two teen girls sharing gossip and complaining about boys, and down one empty seat was a woman with manly features and thick makeup. Belle considered them all with mild amusement, but mostly she was aware of Ian's leg pressing against hers. The automated female voice announced that they were arriving at Westminster, and they stood while waiting for the doors to open.

"Mind the gap," the voice commanded as commuters disembarked, and others hopped on. They moved with the crowd through the brightly lit underground halls, and Belle shivered slightly when Ian pressed his palm against her lower back to guide her.

A tall set of cement steps brought them to street level. Big Ben loomed over them as they walked with the crowd of pedestrians across Westminster Bridge. The Eye stared at her from the opposite side of the River Thames, wide and daunting, like it anticipated her fear and taunted her. She reached for Ian's hand subconsciously for comfort then froze. *What was she doing?* She didn't mean to be so forward.

Belle couldn't bring herself to look up at Ian, afraid of the expression she might find on his face. She closed her eyes and gently pulled her hand away, but Ian's grip tightened.

She glanced up at him then. He smiled and lifted their clasped hands as if to study them. "It's nice," he said. "I like it."

Relieved, she let out a puff of air. "I like it, too."

Her heart went manic as they approached the front of the line, and she was grateful for Ian's hand in hers. She wasn't doing this alone. She was with him, part of something, some*one*, stronger and braver.

Belle tried to distract herself by asking Ian about his life. "What happened to your mum?"

She winced when the words left her mouth. This was what she really wanted to know, but way to jump in with hard personal questions. She couldn't start with something simpler, like his favorite colour or band?

Ian didn't seem to mind, answering without hesitation. "She died in a bus crash when I was eleven. My dad was away a lot with the army so my gran basically raised my sister and me."

Belle glanced at his face and sympathized. Both of his parents dead. "They are in a better place."

Ian rolled a shoulder. "That's what everyone says."

"You don't believe it?"

"I don't know. It seems like the easy way out, though the sentiment is comforting."

"I believe it," Bell said wistfully. "With all my heart. I know I'll see her again someday."

Ian smiled. "I hope you do. What about your dad? What happened to him?"

"I never knew him. I'm not sure mum even knew who he was for sure."

Ian squeezed her hand and Belle searched for a lighter topic. "Tell me about your sister. You said she married an oil baron?"

A slight grimace crossed Ian's face. "Libby's very beautiful, and it was always her goal to use it to her advantage.

Get out of the slums, she used to say. And she succeeded. She lives like a queen and has no use for my gran and me anymore."

"That's too bad," Belle said. So much for lighter topics.

They reached the front of the line and their sad family stories were forgotten. A load of people scrambled into one of the large glass capsules. Belle had seen an ad where a small car had been driven into one, and she felt like she'd just stepped into one of the many science-fiction novels she'd read at the shop. Ian pushed her to the front, and she hung onto a bar on the window. Her hands were sweating and they hadn't even lifted off yet!

The capsule door closed and Belle was glad they were standing far from it. The capsules never actually stop for loading and unloading and she squealed a little as it separated from the platform.

"Are you all right?" Ian asked

"Fine," she squeaked out.

The capsule inched upward and Belle's eyes popped wide as they got farther away from the ground. She gripped the bar with white knuckles.

Ian chuckled. "Are you afraid of heights?"

"I might be."

"Why didn't you say so?"

"I didn't actually know for sure. I've never been higher than the third floor before and in those cases the floor and walls weren't made of glass."

"Well, you're in a pickle then, aren't you? Not like we can get off now."

Ian was joking as the capsule went ever higher, but Belle felt on the verge of tears. She knew she was being irrational. The capsule was enclosed, there was no way she could fall. But what if the actual capsule fell? Twenty people screaming to their deaths in the Thames?

"Oh, Belle," Ian said. "Can I hold you? Would that be all right?"

Belle swallowed and nodded. Mum always told her to look for a silver lining, and having Ian hold her was definitely silver. Bright, shiny, polished silver.

His strong arms wrapped around her from behind and she shivered at his nearness, feeling like she'd just been plugged into an electric socket. She nearly melted when he rested his chin on her shoulder and whispered in her ear. "I promise it's going to be fun."

The ground beneath moved farther away, and Belle forced herself to relax into Ian's firm body. It was the only way she was going to make it through this.

They reached the top of the eye and Ian pointed. "You can see the whole of the Westminster Palace and the top of Big Ben.

"Wow," she said. She'd never seen the city from this perspective before. She hadn't seen anything from this perspective before. She hadn't even flown on a plane. The red, double decker buses looked like toys crossing the bridge. The city spread out like a vast sparkly quilt as far as her eyes could see.

"It's spectacular," she said with feeling. London was grand and beautiful. The sun cracked through the grey sky and sharp fingers of light brightened the city like a jewel. Stunning. Once Belle focused on what she was seeing and not how she was seeing it, she started to really enjoy herself. The Thames, a large, long muddy river ran toward the North Sea, with tugboats and cargo vessels motoring along its banks. All the tourists on the south bank looked like Lego people.

And Ian Connor held her from behind, pressing her back to his chest; it was absolutely fabulous. And best of all, she no longer felt afraid. She felt free!

She was almost sad when the ride ended. "Thank you so much," she said. "That was fantastic."

He wrapped an arm around her shoulders and she reached hers around his waist. "It was a very pleasant experience for me as well," he said with a smirk. "Much, much better than last time when I went up with a bunch of rowdy soldiers."

Ian showed up at King's Books just before closing time the next day. Mrs. Cowen was there so Belle refrained from throwing herself into his arms and laying a good one on him. Not that she'd do that. They hadn't kissed yet, but it was what she continually fantasied about doing.

"So this must be Lieutenant Connor," Mrs. Cowen said. Mrs. Cowen was true to her word and had drilled Belle for details about her date. She was over the moon when she found out Ian was an army man. She walked across the shop and shook his hand. "Oh, you're right, Belle. He really is terribly smashing."

Belle blushed with embarrassment. "Mrs. Cowen."

Ian's lips pulled up in amusement.

"Well, I'll leave you two lovebirds alone," Mrs. Cowen said.

"I'm sorry about her," Belle said after her boss left for the back room. "She reads too many romance novels."

"She seems sweet. I was going to call, but I didn't know if Mrs. Cowen would like it if I did that every day. Are you free after work? My gran wants you to come for dinner."

Belle's heart fluttered. He wanted her to meet his gran? Already?

"Sure," she heard herself say. Just let me say good-bye to Mrs. Cowen and I'll get my coat."

THE ROSE IN THE BRIAR

Anna

Angel whimpered as she pressed her wet nose against Anna's cheek and Anna groaned into her pillow. She had no choice but to rouse her achy body off the couch and walk her dog. "I'm coming," she said, wiping saliva from the corner of her mouth. Her flat had grown dim as the morning turned to afternoon. She reached over to turn on a lamp.

She was already wearing her coat due to her failure to pay the heating bill, so she only had to slip on her boots and attach Angel's leash to her collar. "Just a short one this time, okay?"

If it weren't for Angel, Anna didn't think she'd ever leave her flat anymore. She patted the dog's head. She was probably the reason Anna was still alive.

They strolled slowly around the block, and Anna waited when Angel needed to stop and do her business by the streetlamp. She collected it with the baggy she carried and deposited it in the next bin. The streets were lit with Christmas lights, and many people carried shopping bags filled with gifts. A woman about Anna's age, mid-thirties or so, walked hand in hand with a little girl whose giggles carried across the street. The woman was healthy and pretty... and a mother.

Anna swallowed. She'd missed out on her chance to live that life. Anna hoped the woman knew how blessed she was. Really knew.

Anna tugged on Angel's leash. "Time to go back, girl."

She was so keen on getting back to her flat and more precisely, to her spot on the couch that she forgot to double-check the alley and ran right into her landlord who happened to be leaving as she arrived. Angel barked.

"I don't suppose I'll be seeing rent any time soon?" he growled. No "hello, how are you" noises ever left Mr. Hutchens's mouth.

"I'll get it," Anna said. She wasn't sure how. Maybe she'd sell something. She still had her wardrobe and it was handcrafted from sturdy wood. It must be worth something.

"If you can't afford rent, you can't afford to feed a damn dog." Angel sensed the man's animosity and barked again. Her landlord lurched backward. "It goes, or you go. I ain't no damn charity."

Anna tugged on Angel's leash and huffed as she laboured up the steps to her flat. The man was heartless. Her eyes watered and she rubbed them angrily with the back of her glove. It was like he was asking her to choose between her sofa and her child. She would live on the streets before she gave up her dog.

Anna hung up Angel's leash and refilled her water bowl. She leaned against the counter as she watched the animal drink. Angel followed her back to the sofa. Anna used the last of her energy to pull it out into a full bed. She lay down and patted the space beside her. "Here girl. Let's sleep."

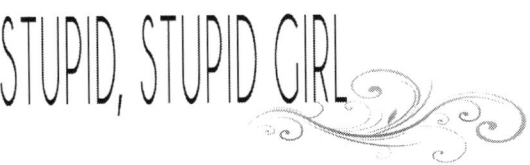

STUPID, STUPID GIRL

Belle

Belle lived a very simple life. Walk to work, walk to the grocers, read books and sleep. She rarely left the London Borough of Barking. All her travels and adventures took place in her imagination. She took public transport when necessary, tubes and buses, but never splurged on a taxi.

She gawked at the black automobile Ian had summoned with his mobile phone. How dull she must be to never have even ridden in a bloomin' taxi? She forced a smile when Ian opened the door, and she crawled into the spacious backseat of the cab.

Belle brushed lint off of her worn jacket and worried. She was poor and unconnected. Couldn't even afford to buy a decent winter coat. What did Ian see in her, anyway? Oh, good Lord, what would his gran think?

"Are you all right?" Ian asked. "You seem tense."

"Just a little nervous."

He nudged her gently. "Gran's a sweetie. No need to worry about her. She'll love you."

Belle nibbled her lip. The truth was she didn't have a lot of love in her life. Her mother had loved her, no question, but other than that? Mrs. Cowen might love her in a friendly way, but she had her own family to love on. Belle lost track of her friends from school, especially during the "sick years." Her mother battled her disease for three years before it took her. Three years that Belle didn't think of anything beside caring for her mother, which meant working at the shop full time and running all the errands, and a long list of nursing duties.

Just thinking about it made her tired.

Ian raised his arm, settling it across her shoulders and squeezed. "I hope this is okay, but you look like you need a hug."

Her face softened. "It's okay." And Ian was right, she did need a hug. She wiggled an arm behind his back and snuggled in until they arrived.

Mrs. Connor lived in a red brick terraced house on a narrow street lined with other identical terraced houses.

"It's number fifty-seven," Ian told the cabbie.

Ian helped Belle out of the taxi, taking her hand. The warmth of his palm against hers, rough over smooth, was both comforting and heart-stopping. She never wanted to let him go, yet knew she had no right to him. And he was leaving again.

This thought filled her with a cool dread, and she forced it back into the "don't touch this" box she kept tucked away in the back of her mind.

Ian poked her playfully in the side. "Relax, will ya?" He opened the door to the terraced house, allowing Belle to go first, and called out, "Gran, we're here."

A door opened to the right, revealing a small living area cluttered with furniture, a television and a bookshelf with lots of non-bookish items. Directly in front to the left was a narrow staircase, which Belle assumed led to bedrooms. Ian's bedroom. She wondered what it looked like.

He led her down a short hall to the kitchen. A row of cupboards lined the back wall, with a window that looked out on a small, frost-covered yard. The appliances included a mint green fridge, a black stove and a white, new-looking washer and dryer set. A rectangle table was pulled away from the wall.

The aroma of fried pork chops filled the place and Belle's stomach woke up. An elderly woman with soft pink cheeks turned towards them while wiping her hands on a blue apron. She had white hair with remnant strands of red pulled back in a short ponytail.

Ian had released Belle's hand just before they'd entered the kitchen and now she was glad of it. Mrs. Connor's brown eyes took her in, a smile appearing on her face a couple moments too late. "Welcome." She shook Belle's hand. "So glad you could make it." She waved to a table that was set for four. "Take a seat."

Ian held out a chair for Belle, giving her a reassuring smile. "Who's the fourth one for, Gran? You find a bloke?"

"Ha, ha," she said. "Those days are over for me, thank God."

A female voice spoke from behind. "It's for me."

Ian swiveled sharply. "Libby?"

"Surprise!" Libby was thin and tall with strawberry-blond hair that hung in long waves over her shoulders. She wore a creamy, silk blouse tucked into crisp trousers with a pressed seam down the front of the legs. Gold earrings hung from her ears and her fingers glittered with bejeweled rings. Her heels clipped across the floor as she walked gracefully to her brother with open arms. "I told Gran not to tell you I was coming. She stepped back holding his shoulders with her hands and took him in. "You look good, Ian. The army must treat you well."

He scoffed a little at that. "You look great, too, Libby, as always."

He turned to Belle. "Let me introduce you to my friend Belle. Belle, my sister, Libby."

Belle felt like she was shaking hands with a model, or movie star or diplomat. Someone so far above her in society Belle wondered if she should curtsy or kiss her hand, or something. "Pleased to meet you," she mustered.

"Likewise." Libby removed her limp hand and sat across from her brother, her eyes never darting to Belle. It was like she wasn't there.

"Where's Shahid?" Ian asked.

Libby rolled her eyes. "He's busy running a corporation. Besides, you know he doesn't do Christmas. I'm only here for a couple days because Gran told me you had leave. Thanks for letting me know, by the way."

Ian shifted uncomfortably. "I don't get a lot of time on the Internet in the field."

Libby rested an elbow on the table and waved salon-perfected fingernails. "How was the field? Anything exciting to report?"

A shadow fell over Ian's face. "I wouldn't call it exciting."

"Oh, boo," Libby said. "There must be something you can tell us. Or is it top secret?"

"Libby, darling," Gran said. "Can you help me bring dinner to the table."

Libby cast Gran a scowl, like she'd asked her to do something her house staff usually did, before reluctantly leaving her chair.

Ian exhaled and shot Belle an apologetic look.

Gran was a good cook, and the pork chops, mashed potatoes and buttery green beans were delicious. Belle had to force herself to slow down.

"So, Belle," Libby began. "I hear you work in a *used* bookstore." Belle had the feeling Ian's sister hadn't stepped foot in any kind of used goods or charity shop in years.

"Yes. There are many volumes to be found in *used* bookstores that can no longer be found in new shops, including valuable first and second-edition books from famed authors."

Libby hummed and tried again. "Are you spending the holidays with family?"

Belle felt like a shrinking doll. "No. I don't have any family."

Libby looked doubtful. "No family at all?"

Belle shook her head.

"You must spend Christmas with us," Gran said. "There's always room for one more."

"Surely, she has friends," Libby said. "People she's known for more than a few days?"

Her eyes darted to Belle. "No offense."

"None taken," Belle whispered, but it wasn't true. She was offended, and her cheeks burned with mortification.

"Really, Libby," Gran said. "Where's your Christmas spirit?"

"I'm an atheist, Gran. You know that. Besides, I'm just pointing out the obvious. She must have someone."

"Libby!" Ian tossed his fork onto the table. "For Pete's sake!"

"I do," Belle blurted. "My boss has me over every year. It's fine, Mrs. Connor. Thanks so much for the offer."

The awkwardness in the small kitchen consumed all the oxygen. Belle struggled to take her next breath.

Gran passed around the bowl of potatoes. "Seconds?"

Belle shook her head. She'd lost her appetite and played with the food that remained on her plate, trying to quiet her heart. She was used to being looked down on, used to having her feelings ignored, but she didn't know how to handle the humiliation she felt with it happening in front of Ian, and by his own sister.

"I forgot I have this other thing I have to do tonight," Belle said, standing. "I hate to eat and run."

Ian pushed his chair back. "Belle?"

"It's okay. I can take a bus to the tube."

"No, I'll call a taxi."

A taxi would mean she'd have to wait around for it to arrive, and she couldn't bear to be there a moment longer. "It's fine, really. Stay with your family." She managed one look back at the two Connor women at the table. "Nice to meet you both."

It was a lie. However, Belle's mother had taught her manners. She forced a smile.

She rushed to put her coat on, but Ian caught up to her before she could make her escape. "Belle, I'm so sorry. My sister…. I wouldn't have brought you here if I'd known."

"It's okay. She's your sister and it's Christmastime. You need to be with them."

"But I *want* to be with you."

He stroked her face and her heart betrayed her. If she were smart, she'd run away and never look back, but she was a stupid, stupid girl. His hand cupped her cheek and she leaned into it.

"Can I come to your place tomorrow?" Ian asked. "Please."

She nodded, unable to deny her heart. "Okay. But you better bring wine."

"I'll do better than that," he said with an effort to lighten the mood. "I'll bring pizza *and* wine."

THE KISS OF THE LOVER

Anna

Except for short excursions to the back alley for Angel's benefit, Anna never left her flat. The kettle whistled and she poured steaming water over a twice-used tea bag. She warmed her hands with the mug as she stared blankly out the window. Snow. It whitewashed the world and at least for a short while, allowed people to imagine that the canvas was clean and could be repainted on.

She spotted a couple walking hand in hand down the street, laughing as they stopped to catch snowflakes with their tongues. She had dark hair sticking out of a winter hat and his was copper brown, shaved short. With strong arms he pulled the girl into an embrace and stared at her, captivated. His mouth landed on hers and he kissed her like the world had fallen away, like the sky had disappeared, like there was no one left in the universe except the two of them.

Anna was unable to look away. Her hand trembled, and she set her teacup on the counter, spilling a little. She gripped the windowsill and watched the couple as they walked away, arm and arm until they turned the corner out of sight.

Anna tasted salt on her lips and realized she was crying. She wiped her face with the sleeve of her housecoat and picked up her cup of tea. It had cooled, but she didn't care.

She returned to her spot on the sofa and called Angel to her side. "What's on TV, girl?" She picked up the remote and flicked through the few channels she could get without cable.

Charlie Brown's Christmas. Wonderful. She'd watch it again. One last time.

TREASURE OF THE SEEKER

Belle

Belle spent the last hour cleaning her flat. It was one open room—kitchen against one wall and a living area that also posed as her bedroom—not an uncommon living arrangement in her neighborhood. The couch pulled out into a sofa bed, but she hadn't bothered converting it to bed form since her mother passed. For her whole life they'd shared the small bed. Belle had folded it back into its sofa form after the funeral and had never pulled it out again. Being rather petite in stature, she was fine with sleeping on the couch. She usually didn't bother putting the bedding away, but today she folded it up and stuffed it in the wardrobe. A small Christmas tree stood in the corner with a few lights and even fewer decorations. Belle always bought the smallest, ugliest tree at the market, the one that she knew no one else would want. It seemed like a charitable thing to do for the tree.

She'd swept and dusted. Covered her small wooden table with a floral tablecloth and lit a half-burned candle that smelled like cinnamon. Then she sat on the edge of the sofa with her hand pushed under her thighs, working to calm the volcanic rush of nerves that bubbled inside her.

Ian was on his way. She was having a male visitor (eek!). A first. She'd never brought boys over when her mother was alive. Belle finally picked up her guitar and started strumming in an effort to distract herself. The instrument was old—it had been her mother's—with nicks and scratches in the rosewood. The strings were in need of changing, but she'd cleaned them recently and that had helped to brighten the tone. She played through several Christmas songs, losing herself enough in the music that she startled at the tapping on the door and squealed like a frightened mouse. Setting the guitar aside, she pushed her hair behind her ears, checked her image quickly in the mirror—barrettes in place, mascara unsmudged—and opened the door.

Ian's face broke into a smile causing his eyes to disappear in the crinkles and Belle couldn't help the smile that spread across her face in response. Steam escaped from the pizza box he held in one hand, and in the other he presented a bottle of red wine.

"As promised."

Belle waved him in. "It's small, I know." She couldn't stop herself from apologizing for her humble flat. "But it's just me."

"It's cozy." Ian placed his goods on the table and removed his coat. Belle gasped a little as she once again took in his army-built physique. Strong arms, broad shoulders, a narrow waist—he looked fantastic in his jeans and a tight long-sleeved T-shirt.

She snapped to attention when Ian caught her staring and quickly retrieved two plates, cutlery and a couple glasses from the cupboard.

"Sorry, I don't have actual wine glasses," she said as she set it all down.

"It'll taste the same no matter the glass."

Ian twisted off the bottle cap and poured. "Did I hear you playing the guitar?"

Belle forgot how thin the doors and walls were in this place. "Oh, yeah."

"You're good. You'll have to play me something."

"I don't know." Belle felt embarrassed. She wasn't used to playing in front of people. She sometimes stopped to watch the buskers in the streets and admired not only their talent, but their courage. She wanted to try it, but so far she was just too chicken. She always dropped a few pence into their open cases to show her appreciation.

"The pizza smells great," Belle said, deftly changing the subject. "What kind is it?"

"I wasn't sure what kind you liked, so I got a deluxe. Is that okay?"

"It's great." Anything that didn't smell like tuna or baked beans—her normal eat-over-the-sink-directly-from-the-tin fare—was great.

She moaned over the cheese as the sharpness exploded in her mouth and the strands stretched from her mouth to the crust in her hand. "So good!"

Ian laughed. "That's what I love about you, Belle. You find joy in the simple things in life."

Belle's face flushed at the use of the word "love," and she hid behind her glass of wine and took a drink.

"I get the impression by the way you refer to your mum that you were close," Ian said in between bites. "Tell me a about her."

Belle's mind drifted back. Her mother used to sit in the very spot that Ian occupied now. "She was kind. Hardworking. She'd wanted to be a nurse, but then I happened, so she never had a chance to finish her training. She cleaned houses instead until she was too weak to do so. She was a good person."

"You miss her, don't you?"

"Yes. It was just the two of us against the world for so long. Now it's just me."

Ian's eyes softened. "I'm sorry for your loss."

"Thanks."

He'd asked her a personal question and now she wanted to ask him one. "I know you don't like to talk about your time on the field in Afghanistan, but was there anything good about it, or was it all…terrible?"

"Mostly it was just boring. And hot. The best part was when we could give something back to the village children. Simple things like pencils would make them smile and laugh. We often handed out water and rice and sometimes we'd get candy to give away, like at Easter time."

"That's nice."

"Yeah. I've been fortunate so far. None of my tours have seen a lot of action, but we hear about the horror and loss of life. I have one more tour to go. I've heard my regiment is going closer to the front this time."

A black inkblot spread across Belle's chest. "When do you go back?"

Sadness flashed behind Ian's eyes. "At the end of the month."

Belle's heart dropped to her shoes. "That's only three weeks away."

He reached across the table and threaded his fingers through hers. "I've learned to live in the moment, Belle. Make each one count. I'm so happy I can spend some of those moments with you."

Belle's emotions ran amok. She finally met someone she really, really fancied, and he fancied her, but he was going to leave her before they even had a chance to get started.

"How long will you be gone?"

"Eight months."

Oh, God. Belle stood, pulling her hand free. She cleaned the table, keeping her eyes averted. This was bad. She was falling for a lad who was on leave. She was so stupid!

She felt the warmth of Ian's hand on her shoulder. "Belle," he said softly. "Look at me."

Belle placed the dishes on the counter and turned slowly. Ian tipped her chin up with his finger and scorched her skin. He ducked down to catch her eyes. "This moment is for us. Let's just enjoy it."

She swallowed and nodded. He leaned in and she thought, *This is it, he's going to kiss me.* Her lips parted, but his mouth skimmed across her cheek, stopping at her ear. "How about that guitar?"

Her knees quivered at his closeness and she was like a snake charmed by the flute of his voice. She couldn't deny him anything. He clasped her hand and led her to the sofa where she'd left her guitar. She propped it across her knees, thankful for the barrier it created. He was too *much,* her attraction to him *too* strong. She had to pull back. Way back. She shifted her body to face him, putting a couple more inches between them.

"I don't know what to play."

"Do you know any Christmas songs?"

"I have one."

Belle fiddled with the tuning pegs, making sure her guitar was in tune, but really she was stalling. Her palms were damp and she quickly wiped them on her jeans. She felt so nervous but not singing it now would cause even greater embarrassment. She closed her eyes and began.

Promise of the prophets
Image of the artist
The hope of the broken
Song of the psalmist
Dream of the mystic
The word of God spoken
Then you sang your song into the world
On that holy Christmas night
Lyric clothed in a flesh of a little babe
Lying in star-light

She stumbled a bit on the second verse. "Sorry. I haven't played it a lot."

"Keep going," Ian encouraged. "It's brilliant."

> *Lord, my eyes have seen the star*
> *You've drawn my heart to behold this child*
> *This light of God who's dawning upon the world*
> *I come to offer him the costly vows of my love*
> *Come all to this palace-barn*
> *This manger-throne*
> *Of the king, the Christ*
> *It's Christmas time*
>
> *Treasure of the seeker,*
> *Reward of the martyr*
> *The voice of the Father*
> *Companion of the loner*
> *The rose to the briar*
> *The Kiss of the lover*

Ian stared at her with wonder in his eyes. The space between them was magnetic, pushing and pulling, reverent with a sense of awe.

"I wrote it as a gift to my mother," Belle whispered. "Our last Christmas together. We didn't have any money to spend on presents."

She couldn't stop the tear that escaped and trailed down her cheek. Ian gently tugged the guitar from her hands and leaned it up against the lone chair beside them. He shuttled closer and drew the pad of his thumb across her wet face.

"Your song is beautiful and so are you."

He tilted his head forward and closed the space between them, his lips hovering over hers. She grabbed the back of his neck, pulling gently, until his lips touched hers. Their kiss was a torch alighting dry leaves. The flames burst from deep within and Belle was enveloped with desire. Nothing else mattered. She *wanted* him. She wanted to *not* feel the pain strangling her heart.

She fell to her back, pulling Ian with her until they were awkwardly horizontal. Ian propped his weight on his forearms, so as not to squish her, but it was the only thing she wanted him to do. Compress her, consume her. His lips trailed moist and hot along her neck to her collarbone and back along her jaw to her mouth. She grabbed frantically at his shirt, pulling it out of his jeans, running searing hot palms along Ian's back. She kissed him like a crazy person, across the ridge of his nose and over the golden scruff on his face. Her hands raced up the curve of his spine, her fingers through his short hair. She arched her back, tugging up her own blouse. Her mind was a smoky haze, her pulse deafening in her ears. All she could think about was Ian's skin and how she wanted to touch every part of him, how she wanted him to touch her.

Their frenzied movements released an earthquake in the room. Belle's guitar tipped over landing on the floor with a bang, the strings ringing out like a foghorn. She snapped back to awareness.

Oh, God! What was she doing? She didn't even know Ian Connor that well. This was what, their second date? Third if you counted the horrible dinner experience with Ian's gran and sister, which she didn't.

Was she about to give it up on a second date? With a guy who was leaving the country in three weeks for half a year?

Belle put two hands on Ian's chest and pushed back gently. She let out several short breaths. "We need to slow down."

She was panting and closed her eyes as she wrestled to gain control. Now she understood her mother's words of caution. "Passion takes over like a hurricane and you won't know what hit you," she had said. "Before you know it, you're staggering through a field of loss and debris. Just be careful."

Ian jumped off the sofa and sprinted to the tiny bathroom, shutting the door. Belle heard the water running in the sink. She sat up, pulled down on her shirt, and smoothed out her hair. She understood now, what her mother had been trying to say. Belle was the result of an intense moment of passion between her mother and a near stranger. She couldn't believe how close she had come to doing the same thing.

Ian eventually returned, his face red and a little damp. He pushed two fists into the front pockets of his jeans and grinned at her. "I'd say I should go home, but I don't really want to."

"I don't want you to, either," Belle said. She patted the sofa beside her. "How about we watch a little telly?"

"Good idea."

Ian sat beside her keeping several inches between them. Belle used the remote to click on the television. "*Charlie Brown's Christmas* is playing," she said. "I love this show."

They'd caught the ending where the kids were putting on the Christmas play.

"That tree looks like yours," Ian said with a grin.

"I love it that way," Belle returned.

Ian placed his palm on the couch face up and nudged Belle with his elbow. She placed her hand in his but didn't dare look at him. She was afraid she'd throw caution to the wind if she did and suffer the consequences later. She pictured her mother's face and stared hard at cartoon Linus as he gave his soliloquy on the true meaning of Christmas.

"'For unto you is born this day in the city of David a savior, which is Christ the Lord. And this shall be a sign unto you. Ye shall find the babe wrapped in swaddling clothes lying in the manger.' And suddenly, there was with the angel a multitude of the heavenly host, praising God and saying, 'glory to God in the highest, and on Earth peace and goodwill toward men.'"

Linus picked up his blanket and walked back to the piano. "That's what Christmas is all about, Charlie Brown."

LYING IN STARLIGHT

Anna

Anna pressed into the frigid wind, thankful that the chemist wasn't too far away. The bell tinkled over the door when she opened it and she welcomed the warm air that greeted her from inside. She pulled the prescription out of her pocket and waited in the queue for the pharmacist.

The short wait gave her a chance to recover from the shivering that had overtaken her body and her fingers prickled as the white tips turned back to pink.

Anna emptied her wallet to pay for the medication when it was ready.

"Merry Christmas," the cashier said as she bagged Anna's purchase.

"Merry Christmas," she replied as she turned to leave.

She heard laughter and conversation from the other side of the aisle. She recognized the warm baritone voice. A peek through the cracks in the shelving confirmed it. *Rhys Williams*. He was with a woman—an in-law?

Anna didn't loiter. The last thing she wanted was for Rhys to see her again, to compare her brokenness with the well-put-together lady at his side. She moved quickly out the door and let out a low breath of relief.

Part of her wanted to go home, just nestle in with Angel and sleep the day away, but another part of her knew she needed to eat and that it would be foolish to pass up a free Christmas dinner. She turned down the side street that led to the soup kitchen.

Anna sighed as she walked through the doors behind two elderly ladies. She'd seen them before on the few times she'd stopped in for the free soup that was offered at noon on weekdays. Anna always felt like a fraud because she wasn't technically homeless. But her cupboards were bare, and that was enough to drive her out on occasion.

The waft of roasted turkey assaulted her immediately and she inhaled deeply. The aroma was heady and her mouth secreted saliva in a way it hadn't in ages.

A long queue had formed. The patrons were all dressed in several layers, and they looked unkempt and worn out. Was that what she looked like? Is that what Rhys saw when he looked at her? Probably. Anna had stopped looking at her reflection in the mirror around the same time her hair started to fall out in clumps in the shower stall.

Anna filled her plate with turkey and cranberries, mashed potatoes and gravy, steamed and buttered brussel sprouts, and picked up a small bowl of Christmas pudding as she searched for a place to sit.

There was an empty seat at the end of one of the tables and Anna slid in. All the bodies and the hot food had heated up the room and Anna felt warm, a sensation she hadn't experienced since the summer. She removed her cap and straightened out the scarf she kept on her head. It didn't hide the fact that she was bald, but it was better than nothing at all. She hated the thought that the lights in the room would reflect off her shiny scalp, and even though she would've liked to take it off, she didn't.

There wasn't a lot of chatter, especially considering how many people were present. Most just focused on what they'd come there to do. Eat.

Anna forced herself to go slow. She wanted to savor every moment, every flavor as it tantalized her tongue and filled her stomach. She felt too full long before she could finish, something she'd anticipated. She slowly tugged on a plastic bag she'd slipped into her pocket for this reason and dumped the remainder of her meal into it. Angel would have Christmas dinner, too.

She poked at her pie and accidentally caught the eye of the older gent across from her. He flashed her a gapped-tooth grin and she smiled back politely.

"Someone should tell 'er that she'll never find a fella if she shaves her head."

It was one of the two elderly women Anna had followed in. Anna suspected they were both hard of hearing and unaware that they talked so loudly to each other.

"Maybe she doesn't want a fella."

"Of course she does."

Anna didn't know if she should laugh or cry. Instead she nodded at the friendly man in front of her and stood to go.

Mr. Hutchens's fat face peered out his window when she turned down the lane to her flat, his permanent scowl directed at her as she approached. He accosted her before she could make it up the steps to her door.

"Your dog barked the whole time you were gone," he snapped.

"I'm so sorry, Mr. Hutchens. I didn't mean to be gone so long."

"I don't care for your excuses. Do something about it, or next time I'll call the pound."

"It won't happen again," she said resignedly. "I promise."

Angel's nose went directly to Anna's pocket when she walked in. Anna poured the contents of the bag into Angel's plastic bowl. "There you go, girl."

It had grown dark and Anna didn't bother to flip the switch. She looked out the window, at a rare winter cloudless night and gazed upon the sliver of the crescent moon in the glow of starlight.

STAY IN THE MOMENT

Belle

Ian picked her up from work and took her out to dinner every night after that. They avoided going up to her flat because Belle thought they both knew what would happen if they did, and even though the idea of *what could happen* appealed to her, it was too risky.

Because the sad, sad truth was that Ian was leaving on New Years Day. Even though she'd known him for only a short while, she couldn't imagine life without him in it. The anticipatory loss injured her in a deep place.

They walked along the main street arm in arm, window-shopping on Christmas Eve. As if sensing her melancholy, Ian pulled her close and spoke into her ear. "Stay in the moment."

He was right. She had plenty of time to be sad in the future. Today she'd be happy. They came upon a fudge shop nestled between a newsstand and a produce shop, and Ian tugged her inside. The sweet aroma was heavenly and the perfect antidote to heavy heartedness.

"What kind do you want?" Ian said. "Chocolate? Rocky Road? Caramel? You pick."

Belle chose butterscotch, and Ian broke the bar in two, handing her half.

Ian stopped them outside the window, and pointed at their reflections as they stuffed fudge into their mouths. "We're a cute couple," he said with a muffled voice.

Belle laughed. "Indeed."

Ian kissed her again. She never tired of his kisses. A million a day wouldn't be too many. His tongue tasted of butterscotch and she feasted on his lips. Her heart swelled a thousand sizes. She'd never been in love before, was never a believer in love at first sight, and though she'd read her share of instant love affairs in the romance novels she read, she thought them to be pure fantasy. No one fell in love that fast.

Yet, here she was after only two weeks, seriously and completely snared.

"Do you want to come up tonight?" she asked. The next day was Christmas and Ian would be spending it with his gran and sister, and so for the first time since they started dating, they'd be spending the day apart.

He smirked. "Do you have a present for me?"

She smirked back. "I might."

"Then yes, absolutely yes!"

Belle didn't know what she'd just promised him, but she didn't care. Even though he was leaving soon, it wasn't like he wasn't coming back. The tour ended in August. He'd be back in the summer. She'd write him letters. He'd write her back. It would be okay.

Stay in the moment, Belle!

They skipped up the snowy steps, and Belle fumbled with the key in her cold fingers. They peeled off their winter coats and Belle put on the tea for warmth.

"I do have a present for you," she said, placing a wrapped gift on the table. It was rectangular and thick, obviously a book. "It's not much."

Ian's dark eyes sparkled as he ripped off the paper. "The last book in the Song of Albion Trilogy. Precisely the right gift." He wrapped his thick arms around her and kissed her. "Thank you."

He rested his forehead on hers. "I have a gift for you but it won't be ready until next week. Sorry, I can't give it to you in time for Christmas."

Belle nudged him playfully. "I didn't expect a present. You don't have to lie. And please, don't get me something just because I got you this. I work at a bookstore. It was nothing."

"I'm not lying. I really have something on order for you."

"Like what?"

"I can't tell you that. It would ruin the surprise."

"Okay, I believe you, because I..." The words burned the tip of her tongue begging to be let go.

Ian drew a line with his thumb along her jaw, a sizzling, blood-warming line. "Because you?" he prompted.

She couldn't hold them back. They insisted on being spoken aloud. "Love you."

Ian's eyes locked with hers and she held her breath. He ran his fingers along the base of her neck and her knees almost gave way.

"I love you, too, Belle. I can't believe it, but it's true. I love you."

IMAGE OF THE ARTIST

Anna

Anna woke to Angel's wet nose nudging her cheek.

"I know, girl," she muttered through dry lips. "You're hungry."

Anna forced herself to rise out of her sleepy haze, went to the bathroom and then dutifully filled Angel's dish with food and changed her water. She scrubbed the animal's ears. "It's Christmas day, Angel. Merry Christmas."

She put on the kettle and fished for a tea bag out of the box. Empty. She groaned. She meant to pick some up the day before but forgot. That was what happened when you slept the day away.

A glance out the window showed a grey sky but no precipitation. "Want to go for a walk?" The dog wagged her tail in a cheery response. "Yeah, let's go for a walk."

PEACE & GOODWILL

Anna didn't bother to get dressed, just slipped on her winter jacket over her pjs and tucked the pajama pants into her boots. They were red with white polka dots, fitting enough for the holiday.

They headed in the direction of the Asian specialty food shop. They sold the best green tea at the best prices—Anna fingered her last pound coin in her pocket—plus, they were Hindus, which meant they stayed open on Christmas day.

Anna spotted a man sitting along one of the shops that was closed for the holiday. He had brown skin, long black dreads and a large dog curled up beside him. A can for coins sat out in front by his feet.

"Nice dog," he called out as Anna attempted to walk by.

Anna stopped. "Thanks. You too."

The man patted the top of his dog's head. "His name is Byron."

"This is Angel," Anna returned.

"Hey, Angel," the man said. Angel tugged on her leash wanting to go to the man. Anna relented and took a step closer. Angel and Byron sniffed each other, and the man patted Angel's head.

"Great name," he said. "Byron is my guardian angel. Saved my life more than once. Sleeping in the streets ain't the safest thing, y'know. He's great for keeping a man warm in the winter, too."

"Where are you from?" she asked. The man's accent wasn't local.

"Barbados. Came to London looking for a better life." He chuckled humourlessly. "Landed on hard times recently."

"Times are tough," Anna admitted.

"I'm James by the way." The man stood and offered a hand.

"Anna." She kept her gloves on but shook his hand anyway. She noticed red cracking lines crawling across his dark skin from the cold. "Nice to meet you."

"Are you a Londoner?" James returned to his seat on a worn, dirty piece of cardboard on the pavement.

"Lived here all my life," she answered. "I hear Barbados is beautiful."

"Ah, it is so," James said with dark, dreamy eyes. "White sand, warm sunshine, ocean water as clear blue as the Queen's crystal."

Anna sighed. "Sounds lovely. You must be homesick."

"Oh, so much so. My family…" James's eyes grew glassy. "Once I have enough money saved, I'm going home." He eyed her. "I don't suppose you could spare some change?"

Anna wasn't surprised by the solicitation. The empty can sat like a beacon between them.

She gripped the coin in her pocket with her fist. "Sure." She tossed it in the jar. "Merry Christmas. I hope you can get home soon."

"Thank you, miss, and Merry Christmas to you!"

Anna called for Angel and headed back home without her tea, yet she felt strangely warm inside despite it.

IT'S CHRISTMASTIME

Belle

All alone on Christmas day? What was she thinking?

Belle's eyes burned with tears and she pressed cool palms up against them. She should've gone to Mrs. Cowen's again. Thinly veiled tolerance from her daughter and grandkids was better than complete isolation. She thought she could do this, thought she was stronger. A hollow pit grew in her gut.

She turned on the telly, but all the happy Christmas television families just added to her melancholy. She clicked it off and pulled her duvet over her head like a turtle in its shell, blocking out the pain and loneliness with the stale-smelling darkness.

Her heart longed for her mother. Holidays were the worst times and Christmas the very worst of the worst. The pain twisted unbearably. She snuggled deeper into the darkness in a futile attempt to escape it.

Mercifully, she fell into a dreamless slumber only to be awakened late afternoon by a tapping on her door. She threw her blanket off her face and winced as the light accosted her face. The tapping returned.

"Just a minute," she called out. Who could it be? Surely her landlord wouldn't choose Christmas day to deliver a complaint. And there was no way he'd be stopping by to drop off gifts. That hadn't happened in the eight years she'd lived there, and it wasn't bound to happen now.

Belle ran fingers through her hair, not that it helped to erase her disheveled look. She wished she'd put in a little more effort when she saw the person standing on the other side of her door.

"Ian? What are you doing here?"

He blew in with a wall of cold air and scooped her up into his arms. "Merry Christmas to you, too."

Belle flushed with embarrassment and covered her face. "I'm a mess. Why didn't you tell me you were coming?"

"Well, first off, you're adorable. And second, didn't you tell me you would be at the Cowen residence today?"

Belle nibbled her lip. Not much she could say to that. She was caught in a flat-out lie. "I didn't want you to feel bad for me."

"I thought something was up. You're not a very good liar, you know, in case you've considered making a career out of it, so I asked Mrs. Cowen about you when you were busy with a customer. She told me that you said you had other plans this year."

Belle groaned and flopped into a kitchen chair. "This is so embarrassing. I just didn't want her, or you, to feel like you had an obligation to me. It's just one stupid day of the year. I can manage on my own for one day."

Ian's eyebrow jumped. "You look like you're managing well. Now go shower and get dressed. I'm taking you to the cinema. Something really cheesy and romantic and …" he grinned mischievously. "I expect a lot of snogging to be going on between us so don't miss out on your toothbrush either."

The day was suddenly brighter, and Belle hurried to do as told. There was nothing she'd rather do with the rest of her day than snuggle in a dark room and snog with Ian.

When she exited the shower, Belle was stunned to smell the savory aroma of meat pie baking in her oven. The table had been set for two and a bowl of fruit sat in the middle. "What's this?"

"We can't go to the cinema on an empty stomach, can we? I can't chance you being distracted by a growly belly."

"I didn't see a bag of groceries."

"I left them on the doorstep. I wanted to surprise you."

"You succeeded in your mission. I'm surprised."

With a full stomach and warm heart Belle walked with Ian to the neighbourhood cinema. She grabbed onto his arm to save herself from slipping on the ice and didn't let go. The sky had darkened to a moody purple and the street lamps flickered on. The only thing that could make the evening even more perfect was snow.

"Is anything even playing on Christmas day?" she asked.

Ian nodded. "Oh yeah. It's a big money-making day for movies."

Belle didn't know that. She never had extra money on Christmas to spend, so she hadn't explored the option. "What's playing?"

Ian named a new action film with the latest British hotshot star and a romantic drama.

"Oh, hard choice," Belle said with a tease in her voice.

"Normally, I'd see the action flick," Ian admitted. "But, today I'm looking for something quieter."

"You mean boring."

He laughed. "You said it, not me."

"There's nothing wrong with a little romance," she insisted.

Without slowing, he turned and kissed her head. "I'm counting on that."

Belle heard the strumming of a guitar as they turned the corner, and they slowed as they approached a street singer standing in front of the train station. A dark-skinned woman dressed in a shabby jacket and mismatched hat and scarf played the instrument while wearing white fingerless gloves. Her voice was angelic and rang out boldly through the near empty streets.

PEACE & GOODWILL

Silent night, Holy night
All is calm, all is bright
Round yon virgin, mother and child
Holy infant, so tender and mild
Sleep in heavenly peace,
Sleep in heavenly peace.

Silent night, Holy night
Shepherds quake, at the sight
Glories stream from heaven above
Heavenly, hosts sing Hallelujah.
Christ our Savior is born,
Christ our Savior is born.

Belle's breath hitched at the beauty of the song. Her gaze landed on the grocery cart behind the woman filled with sundry items that didn't include food and Belle knew she was homeless. She sighed as she searched her pockets for spare change but came up empty.

Ian stepped towards the woman and dropped a couple bills in her guitar case.

"Thanks, mister," the woman said with a broad, sincere smile. "Merry Christmas."

"Merry Christmas to you, too," he said.

They continued on at a relaxed pace, hand in hand. Belle felt her mouth stretch into a smile. Clearly making it to the cinema on time wasn't a priority.

She felt something damp drop on her face and looked up. "Snow," she whispered. You had to look under the cone of light coming from the street lamp to see how fat and fluffy the flakes were as they floated to the ground, deadening the sound around them.

"It's a snow shower," Belle said.

Ian dragged her under the lamp and grinned. "We must shower in it together."

He tilted his head down, and she stood on her tiptoes reaching for his neck. The heat of his lips sizzled against her frozen ones and she took him in with a satisfied sigh. This was the best Christmas ever.

NEW YEAR'S EVE

Anna

The pounding in Anna's head competed with the pounding on the door to her flat. She pressed cold fingertips against her temples. *Please, could the world just quiet down?*

Whoever was knocking on the door was persistent. It could be only one person. Anna sighed and swallowed two pain-relief capsules before calling out, "I'm coming."

She padded to the door in stocking feet and pulled her sweater tight across her diminished bosom. "Hello, Mr. Hutchens."

"Rent's due and it's up fifty pounds."

"Fifty pounds?" Anna had sold everything she owned except the sofa. Her wardrobe, table and chairs, even the television was picked up a day ago. Despite it all, she had fallen short and now with the rent increase, there was no way she could cover it.

"This is all I have." She held out her cash and Mr. Hutchens counted it. "I need one hundred pounds more."

"I don't have it."

"Then you're out."

"Out?"

"Yes." Mr. Hutchens raised his voice. "Out!"

Angel growled.

Anna gulped. She'd lived in this flat for sixteen years. She'd witnessed Mr. Hutchens' hairline recede and his waistline thicken. "Where am I supposed to go?"

"Not my concern. I'm not a bloody charity. New renters want to move their things in tomorrow morning. You better be out or I'll get the coppers to toss you."

Mr. Hutchens huffed down the back stairs with Anna's money firmly in his gritty hand.

"Hey," she called. "I want my money back."

Mr. Hutchens scowled and shook his fist full of bills. "This is for last month."

Anna slowly closed the door and inched back to the sofa in a daze. She collapsed and fought back tears. Angel moaned and rested her chin on her lap.

"It's okay," Anna said, patting the dog's head. "The shelter will take us for a few nights and they don't mind a well-behaved dog. I just need time to get things sorted."

A few days to find her best friend a new home. Anna wrapped her arms around the animal's warm, furry neck. "Love you, girl."

PEACE & GOODWILL

With her guitar in one hand and Angel on the leash in the other, Anna took one last look at her near-empty flat before closing the door forever. Outside the sky was a dark, broody grey. Snow fell in chaotic swirls, whipped and dropped by a brisk, cold wind. Anna leaned into it, pressing her chin into the wool scarf around her neck. The shelter wasn't far, but when she approached she groaned. The queue to get in for the night was a mile long. They only had so many beds, and once they were filled, the latecomers were sent away until the doors opened again for breakfast the next morning.

She went to the front of the queue to inquire. "Are there enough beds?"

The lady taking names took a moment to peer down the line. "Not likely."

"What am I to do then?"

The woman sighed. "Most people find shelter from the elements under the bridge. Your dog will protect you. Get here early in the morn, and I'll make sure you're on the list for tomorrow night.

Anna thanked the lady and called Angel's name. She started for the river but somehow ended up at the cemetery.

THE GIFT

Belle

It was Ian's last day before leaving in the morning for his final tour and Belle had wanted to take the day off. Unfortunately Mrs. Cowen insisted that she couldn't spare her. The holidays were busy and she needed her help. At least the shop closed early.

"Belle, dear," Mrs. Cowen said, "Can you hang this up outside for me? I'd ordered it ages ago, and it finally came. You can put the old sign in the trash and hang this one up in its place."

Belle removed the object in question from the packaging. It was a rectangular metal sign with embossed lettering painted gold that said: *Find the Great Escape in Books*. Somehow, despite the cold against her fingers, she managed to replace the old sign which had simply said *Used Books*. She did whatever Mrs. Cowen asked of her as quickly as possible. She needed to keep busy; otherwise, she'd spend the whole time watching the clock, and the seconds always crawled by when she did that. Finally the day ended, and she hurried home to get ready for Ian.

Belle's stomach was in so much upheaval, she felt like she was going to throw up every five minutes. She'd showered and had been dressed and ready for the last half hour, pacing a hole in the floor as she waited for Ian to arrive.

She sprinted to the door and swung it open before he'd finished knocking. She ignored his shocked expression and the wrapped box in his arms, pulled him inside and attacked his face with her lips. She wanted to gobble him up, ravage him, tie him down and never let him go.

"Whoa," Ian said, laughing. "You're squishing my present."

Belle thought she heard a squeak come from the box. "Is that my late Christmas present? Did it just make a noise?"

Ian swung a bag on the table. "Wine. For later. And yes to answer both your questions."

Belle's eyes widened as Ian handed her the gift. It was heavy and she could feel movement. That was when she noticed two holes in the box. Air holes.

"Ian…"

"Just open it."

Belle ripped off the wrapping paper and removed the lid. Inside was a little puppy. "He's so cute!"

"She," Ian corrected. "It's a girl."

"Oh, Ian. My landlord will never agree to let me keep her. He's a real stickler when it comes to pets."

"He and I had a little chat. He's agreed to make an exception this once."

"You paid him off?"

Ian laughed. "Yeah." He draped an arm around her shoulders and gently petted the animal. "I didn't want to leave you alone. I thought she could keep you company until I got back."

Belle's heart almost exploded. "I love you so much! It's going to be the longest eight months of my life, but this little girl will definitely help." She held the puppy up to her face and squealed when her little pink tongue ran a wet line across her cheek. "Good thing there are a lot of books on puppy care at the store," she said through a broad smile, "because I really don't have the first clue."

"You'll figure it out," Ian said. He poured two glasses of wine and led Belle with her present to the couch. The puppy snuggled on her lap and fell into a deep puppy sleep.

Belle leaned into Ian and kissed his neck. "You are amazing."

"As are you." He tapped his glass to hers. "Here's to the best New Year's ever."

Belle sipped her wine and then, careful not to disturb the precious pup on her lap, she tilted her head back and waited for Ian's soft, warm lips.

PEACE & GOODWILL

Stay in the moment.

There were moments in Belle's life that she wished she could freeze. Turn them into paper cutouts, fold them, put them in envelopes and tie them with ribbon and never let them go.

Like the first time she baked a cinnamon cake. Or got an A+ on her English paper and how Mr. Oswell praised her work in front of the whole class. The last Christmas she spent with her mother.

This moment right now. Kissing Ian good-bye at the front entrance of the Barking train station. Tears ran down her cold, red cheeks, but she didn't bother wiping them away. Her arms tightened around Ian's neck as she consumed his lips.

Stay in the moment.

Ian's embrace tightened until she felt she couldn't breathe. She didn't want to breathe. She didn't want to live through the part where they had to say good-bye.

"I love you, Belle."

Belle choked back a sob. It bubbled in her chest, a mounting volcano she couldn't contain. It escaped with her response, "I love you, too."

She sobbed into the rough canvas of his army jacket. The puppy at the end of the leash yelped as she sensed Belle's heightened emotion and bit at her heels.

Belle forced a laugh and bent to swoop her up. "She feels left out."

"It's only eight months," Ian said. "It'll pass before you know it."

Her eyes burned and leaked like miserable old taps.

Ian cupped her wet cheeks in his rough hands. "I want to memorize your face. I'll take this memory of you, of this moment, and fall asleep with you on my mind. When I wake up, it'll be you that I think of. You will get me through the monotony of the day."

He kissed her again and Belle devoured his lips. *Stay in the moment.* This was Ian's body pressed against hers, his lips on her lips, his cheeks brushing against hers.

Stay in the moment.

She hated this moment. *Hated* it. She didn't want to say good-bye, didn't want to let him go.

"Ian," she whimpered.

"Shh. It's going to be okay." He glanced at his watch and frowned. "I have to go. I can't miss this train."

"I know," she said.

Ian grabbed her one last time and kissed her softly on her forehead. "Until we meet again, my love," he whispered.

He walked backwards towards the station, the invisible band that held them stretching, crying, calling until he disappeared from her view.

Snap.

She ran home awkwardly through the grit piled up on the pavement, the puppy pressed to her face covered in hot, messy tears.

Good-bye, Ian.

I'VE MISSED YOU

Anna

Anna pushed against the cemetery gates. She hadn't been there in a couple of years and without thinking about the damage it would do to her heart, she entered the grounds.

    Early dusk threw a low angle glow that reflected an ethereal pink and blue across the snow. She stopped when she reached the headstone she was looking for. Her knees trembled, from the cold or something deeper, she wasn't sure, and she fumbled with the frosty snaps on her guitar case.

    Anna strapped the instrument over the thick shoulders of her winter coat and played with the tuning pegs until the strings tightened in tune. Angel sat obediently at her side, waiting for the song to come like she had a thousand times before.

> *Treasure of the seeker,*
> *Reward of the martyr*
> *The voice of the Father*
> *Companion of the loner*
> *The rose of the briar*
> *The kiss of the lover*

She sang to the man whose name marked the grave. Lieutenant Ian Connor, September 19, 1981-August 9, 2006. When she finished the song, she knelt down and ran her finger over her love's name.

"I can't believe it's been eight years since I kissed you good-bye."

Anna's fingers burned from the cold as she packed away her guitar. Her heart hurt, too, but not as bad as last time she visited. The sharp brittle pain had numbed to something softer and manageable and though her eyes felt watery, not one tear escaped.

She stumbled towards the gates. Her head pounded and she found it difficult to walk, vaguely aware that her gait and motion resembled a drunkard. Angel barked. People passed her by, giving her odd and disapproving stares. She was half a block away from the graveyard when her foot lodged on a stone and she fell.

Pain exploded in her head and she cried out.

Then it was gone. In its place was light. A bright light, warm and comforting. She felt herself reach for it. So beautiful and comforting. Her heart knew it was the light of God.

A woman's face appeared in the whiteness. "It's okay, darling. I'm here now."

"Mummy?"

Her mother's face was young and her cheeks a rosy, healthy red. "Yes, my sweets," she said gently. "It's me."

Anna groaned as her consciousness pulled her back. The cold wind whipped her face. Her ankle throbbed. Snow fell softly on her eyelids. She closed them, longing for the bright light to return, to stroke her and erase the fear.

"It's me, love, wake up."

Her eyes opened once again to the gentle light. Ian, *her Ian*, stood beside her. Her heart jumped. "Is it really you?"

"It is. I've missed you."

"I've missed you, too. So much."

He extended his hand and she took it, and suddenly she was on her feet. She noted how her skin was no longer grey and loose on her bones, but firm with a healthy pinkish glow. Instead of winter rags, she wore a lovely, white dress. Her dark hair hung in waves along her face. She felt energetic and free, and more alive than ever before.

Ian wrapped his arms around her and smiled. "We meet again," he said, "like I told you we would." She smiled back, her heart filled with the warmth of love that spanned all the years they'd been apart, pulling tightly as if time never existed, a mere time in between times. Like they'd never really parted ways.

TIME IN BETWEEN TIMES

Annabelle

Annabelle Vaughn looked down at the body of a woman covered in snow. A dog, her Angel, pressed her furry body along the woman's side in a vain effort to keep her warm. Angel whimpered and nudged her owner's cheek.

A man passed by and Angel barked, standing but refusing to leave her owner's side.

Annabelle knew the man. Handsome with greying hair and lines around friendly hazel eyes.

"What is it, mate?" the man asked. He bent low, staring at the dog's face and said, "Angel?"

Angel barked.

"Angel, where's Anna?" That was when he spotted the form, just beyond the animal, covered in snow. "Oh, no." He rushed to the body, shook it and listened for breath. He pulled a mobile out of his pocket, dialed 999 and reported his find.

Annabelle turned to Ian. "Why am I seeing this?"

He stroked her hair and let his head fall forward until it touched hers. "You can go back."

"What do you mean?"

"It's not your time if you don't want it to be. Belle, go back. Live your life."

"What about you?"

"I'll always be here." He tapped the spot above her heart. "And here."

Annabelle heard Angel whine as if the sound came through a long tunnel. Ian gently pulled out of her arms. "Good-bye, Belle." His voice grew distant. Her vision darkened.

"Anna!"

Pressure pounded on her chest as she heard Rhys's voice counting: five, six, seven, eight, nine, ten. One, two, three… She gasped and her burning lungs filled with icy air.

"Anna? Oh, Anna!"

Her eyes popped open and Rhys's concerned face filled her view.

"You're going to be all right, love," he said. "Help is on the way."

He pulled her onto his lap and rubbed her frozen hands until the police and ambulance arrived. "I'll meet you at the hospital," he told her as the paramedics lifted her onto the gurney. "You aren't alone."

With a low raspy breath she asked, "What about Angel?"

"Don't worry about her, love. She'll be with me. I'll take good care of her. Don't you worry about anything."

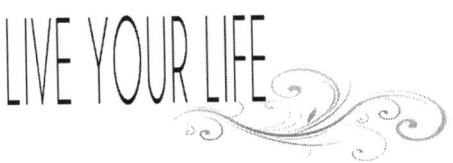

LIVE YOUR LIFE

Rhys

Rhys Williams was a widower. He'd met his wife in uni, fallen deeply in love and married her the first summer after graduation. His family was well off and he and Myra had enjoyed everything life had to offer: enriching careers, he an engineer, she a school administrator, lots of travel, a nice house on an acreage north of London. They had two daughters who brought them both immense joy, though the teen years were a little difficult. Still they'd turned out well. The oldest one Janie married an Irish lad and lived in Dublin with a wee one still in nappies. The youngest one Bette was traveling in America.

They kept in touch but the reality was he didn't see them very often. Everyone was so busy.

Rhys considered moving out of the big house after Myra died. There were so many memories at their home that pained his heart unbearably.

It was also those very memories that had prevented him from selling. Still, the place was lonely and so terribly quiet. It was why he had agreed to go to Barking to visit Myra's family for the holidays. It was Janie's husband's turn to have Christmas with his family and Bette was staying with people she met in California. Rhys didn't relish spending the holidays alone.

Myra's family was financially poorer than his own, but they were rich in many ways that counted far more. The holidays spent with them were pleasant. But the most surprising thing, the most precious thing that came from that vacation was Annabelle Vaughn. It was fortunate timing that he'd gone to visit Myra's grave just as Anna had collapsed in the snow.

She and Angel had stayed in his guest house since the moment she'd been released from hospital. At first she refused his offer of accommodation stating she had no way to repay him, but just filling this place with life and conversation was payment enough for him.

The warmth of early spring filled the garden behind his vine-covered brick home. Rhys brought a tray with tea and biscuits out to where Anna sat at a wrought-iron patio table in the sun, a soft rug folded over her lap. Angel lay in a tired, contented heap near her feet.

"Here you go, love," he said while pouring for her.

She looked up at him kindly. "Thank you, Rhys." She spooned in one teaspoon of sugar and stirred before taking a careful sip.

Her hair had grown in a little, but it was short like a pixie's, and her dark eyebrows had returned enhancing her beautiful green eyes. The doctors couldn't explain her recovery. It happened sometimes to people who had a near-death experience, they said. It was a scientific mystery. Rhys's minister called it a miracle.

Over the course of their weeks spent together Rhys had told Anna all about his happy years with Myra, and Anna had shared about her soldier. It seemed unfair that he had years of memories with his first love where Anna had only a few weeks.

A warm breeze stirred and the floral scent of spring blossoms filled the air. Anna breathed it in and Rhys was pleased to see the rosy flush in her cheeks. Her eyes sparkled with life in a way he hadn't witnessed before.

"Perhaps, if the weather holds, we can go into London," Rhys said. "We could see a play or a concert if you'd prefer. My treat."

"It's always your treat," she said with a hint of chastisement. "I'm not sure that's fair."

Rhys knew Anna was concerned about the imbalance of wealth between them. She had nothing in the form of monetary value to bring to their friendship—their relationship—but she had so much more. "Your company is a treat to me," he said with a smile, hoping to encourage her.

Annabelle may have lacked earthly riches, but she was rich in so many other ways. She was strong, determined, kind and thoughtful. Yes, she was young, at least fifteen years his junior, but she was mature beyond her years. A hard life made a person grow up quickly.

His admiration ran deep.

Truth was, he more than admired her. During these past three months he'd fallen in love.

A flush of happiness swirled through his being at the thought, immediately followed by a disconcerting thud in his chest. What if these feelings only flowed one way? Was it possible Annabelle Vaughn felt for him the love that had sprouted in his heart for her? Or did she simply see him as a middle-aged man with a generous heart who helped a poor girl out in a time of need? Or worse, did she see him as the lonely, old guy that he was?

Anna's expression tightened with concern as she watched him. She reached over and covered his hand with hers. "Is everything all right?"

His gaze settled on their hands. Her skin was so soft, her fingers so very delicate.

His eyes met hers. "That would depend on you."

"Oh?" Anna said.

Rhys shuffled his chair closer, then took both of her hands in his. "What I mean is I want you to stay with me. Forever. I love you Annabelle. I'm hoping that you're feeling something for me. Even a little. Enough to say yes. Enough that you might see yourself one day as my wife."

Tears welled up behind Anna's eyes. "Oh, Rhys, are you sure? I don't know how long I have on this earth. Do you really want to take that chance?"

Rhys reached up and gently stroked her chin. "Darling, no one knows the number of their days. All we can do is live each new one we have to its fullest. I want to spend every new day with you."

Anna laughed and cried and laughed again.

Rhys grinned back at her. "Can I interpret your response as a yes?"

Anna smiled brightly. "Yes. Yes, you can."

He leaned in close and whispered in her ear, "In that case, would it be okay if I kissed you?"

Anna simply nodded.

Rhys closed the gap between them and rested his lips gently on hers. They were soft and moist and his whole body trembled as he took her in. He tasted the saltiness of her tears on her cheeks and kissed each one away. She pressed her lips to his neck and said softly, "I never thought I could be so happy again."

He held her close, hardly believing this wonderful, beautiful woman agreed to be his. "Neither did I, darling. Neither did I."

The End

To hear about new releases and promotions, sign up for Lee's newsletter at leestraussbooks.com.

If you enjoyed reading *Peace & Goodwill*, please consider leaving a review. Reviews are very helpful to Indie authors and help readers discover the books they love.

Please enjoy this sample from
EAST OF THE SUN
By Lee Strauss

Regret is a formidable foe.

Regret: to feel sorry about an event, one's acts, etc.; remorse, esp. over one's acts or omissions.
Formidable: causing fear, dread or awe; hard to handle.
Foe: an enemy.

Eden always imagined an enemy to be living, breathing and covered with flesh, like Lisa Putnik who was uber-popular in high school, and was threatened by Eden because she'd won the heart of the new boy; or her former boss in the northern town of Landers, the fat old fart who would've fired her if she hadn't quit first. Or Revenue Canada.

But not regret. That was a soulish emotion that could be readily brushed off and forgotten in a day or two.

Or so she'd once thought.

Chapter One

1990

Eden hesitated before knocking. She stood on the wooden porch of her childhood home with her four-year-old daughter Sophie leaning sleepily against her. She was struck by the uncharacteristic neglect of the property. The vines on the trellis needed trimming, as did the hedges and the lawn. Patches of stucco had come loose and lay in the sun-bleached grass. She had to dodge a sizable web of silk to get to the door.

Often in recent years she had dreamed of this moment, but now, with the imminent inquisition by her mother at hand, her courage waned. In her mind, her mother remained younger, well, if you considered middle age younger, with a spring to her step. She would answer the door while wiping her wet hands with the white apron that covered her skirt, smoothing the wrinkles out.

And she'd be smiling. She smiled a lot back then, though Eden's memories have become plastic, her mother's face morphing into a less natural, mannequin-like image.

Eden breathed deeply and knocked. She waited for the soft steps of her mother, but none came. A second and third knock brought no answer. She rang the bell. Mom must be out, she thought. Serves me right for not calling first.

She tried the knob and the door swung open.

"Mom?"

Only an eerie quiet. Eden directed Sophie to the sofa where she embraced a cushion and promptly fell asleep. The long drive back to Vancouver had worn the little girl out.

The living room looked much the same as it did when Eden came home three years earlier for her father's funeral, but it lacked the precise tidiness she remembered. She moved on to the kitchen, giving it a cursory glance as she passed through, noting the dirty pots and dishes littering the counters. A flare of concern flashed through her. Uncleanness was not in keeping with her mother's character.

Several old pizza boxes were stacked on the table. A foul smell lingered, and Eden plugged her nose, following it to its source: a stack of partially emptied cat food tins behind a cupboard door. Beside them sat a small hill of unopened tins. Eden now hoped that her mother had recently acquired a cat. The back door, which led to the porch and then to the object of her mother's obsession, the flower gardens, stood wide open.

Eden was now thoroughly concerned. These gardens, once beautiful, exact and Eden's main competitor for her mother's affections, were now nothing more than a tangle of humiliation, like an aging movie star whose beauty was ravished by substance abuse.

Eden took a timid step forward, fighting against choking uneasiness. She pushed back unruly branches to enable a clear passage, and plodded on.

She was distraught by her discovery. An old woman, vaguely familiar, but surely a trespasser, bent over a brittle, helpless rose bush. She snipped violently with a pair of rusty clippers. Her white hair was short and choppy. Several layers of clothes hung from her thin frame. Rose buds lay strewn across the ground, their fragrance and beauty cut short and left to wither and die in the summer heat.

"Mom? Is that you?"

The woman's eyebrows furrowed in question, deep lines pressing a V over her nose. "Well, for goodness sakes, Lillian, Help me up!"

Eden scrambled to assist her as the woman babbled on. "Where on earth have you been? I've waited and waited for you. You went on that cruise with Mr. Kipper, didn't you? I knew you would go and leave me behind." She pulled away angrily and stormed off toward the house.

"Where is Joshua?" she continued, "Has he returned from the sea? They fish for days and days, one loses track. Is he home?"

The pit in Eden's stomach tightened. She had a nebulous mental file about her father, Josh Emerson, working as a fisherman while a young man. He'd been a successful architect for as long as she could remember until he retired one year prior to his heart attack.

She joined her mother on the back porch where they were greeted by a number of stray cats. Eden was relieved her mother wasn't the consumer of the stash of cat food she had discovered.

"Why don't I get us something cold to drink?" Eden said while guiding her mother to a vacant, weather-worn rocking chair.

"Don't put any ice in mine, Lillian," she said. "You know how it bothers my teeth."

Eden sucked on a cigarette like a diver low on oxygen, and stared through the window at the stranger on the porch. She'd decided she would quit smoking when she made plans to move back to Vancouver to start fresh and new on all fronts, but that resolution would have to wait. After butting out, she checked on her sleeping daughter, then poured two glasses of water, one without ice, and carried them outside.

Eden wasn't the only one at a loss for words. Her mother rocked in her chair causing a rhythmic creak, not bothered by the fly buzzing loudly around them.

What was wrong with her? Eden thought. Did she go into shock since dad's death? Did she spend too much time in the sun? Did she hit her head?

Eden thought guiltily, that she should have come home sooner, but it was such a long drive, and the truth was she and her mother rarely saw eye to eye.

"I'm still sore at you," her mother finally muttered. "How could you leave me like that? All alone. You know I don't like to be alone."

"I'm sorry. I should've come home sooner, I know."

Her mother lifted a shoulder. "It's okay, Lil."

Why did she keep calling her that? "I'm Eden. Mom." She waited for a response, an acknowledgement of a simple slip of the tongue, but got none. "Where is Aunt Lillian, anyway?"

When her mother didn't answer, she tried a different tactic. "Look, you're probably wondering why I'm here without Cade. Well, you're not going to like it. We split up." Eden waited for the expected disapproving frown. A cluck of the tongue. Eyes that widened with concern and curiosity, but her mother's expression remained blank.

"Mom? Did you hear me? I just told you that Cade and I have separated."

Eden pulled another cigarette out of her blouse pocket. Her mother's behaviour should have caused her to be overcome with worry for her mental health, but instead Eden fought back anger. She knew she was being unreasonable, but her mother was never there for her. Had never been there. She had hoped things could be different this time.

When her mother finally spoke, she made no sense at all. "Why did you go on that cruise without me? What will the neighbours think if they find out you've gone off alone with Mr. Kipper like that? It's dreadful." She worried her bony hands on her lap. "Oh where is Josh? Is he home?"

Eden tossed her cigarette onto the porch and squashed it with her sandal. After a second thought she picked it up and placed in on the table.

"I'm going inside to call a doctor, and then I have to wake up Sophie, or she'll never go to sleep tonight."

She reached over and laid her hand on the elderly woman's shoulder. "Everything's going to be okay. I'm here now."

Chapter Two

Eden moved up north with Cade immediately after graduation almost six years ago, much to her parents chagrin. She had only been back once, for her father's funeral, and had lost touch with her friends. She needed a referral to a good doctor because her mother's doctor was booked solid for a week. The situation seemed too urgent to wait.

Eden recalled a girlfriend from high school, Marti Rae. They hadn't been best friends or anything, but she lived nearby and had met her mother before. She looked up her number in the phone book and dialed.

"Hi, Marti?"

"Yeah, who's this?" Marti had the smoothest radio voice and Eden wasn't surprised when she was hired on as a DJ with a local radio station. Behind the suave voice was a very ordinary, wallflower type of girl. A little overweight with thick glasses, she hadn't been popular with the boys back in high school.

"It's Eden."

"Eden Emerson?"

"Yeah, well, Eden Kelley now."

"Of course, I was at your wedding. Just slipped out. Habit I guess. Are you in town?"

"Just arrived today."

"Oh, that's great. Good to hear from you."

"Uh, yeah, you, too. The reason I'm calling is my mom's not feeling well and I want to take her to a new doctor, you know, get a second opinion? And your name came to mind. Could you give me a referral?"

Ten minutes later, Eden hung up the phone from a call with Dr. Sue Chan's office. Lorraine Emerson had an appointment the next afternoon at 2:15

Eden returned to the back porch and leaned on the doorsill, arms crossed.

"So, this is some kind of surprise for both of us, isn't it?"

Lorraine smiled sweetly, her mouth twitching slightly, but she said nothing.

Inwardly, Eden bemoaned the fact that her mother was obviously too ill to babysit Sophie so she could restart her life. She expected adamant objections to her decision to leave Cade. Eden had a defense speech memorized, ready to dish out. She and Cade had nothing in common. She missed the city, and though he said he did, too, he seemed to be quite at home in the country. He liked the logging, hunting and skidooing culture. "When in Rome..." he'd say. And, "It won't be forever, just until we can afford to move back." But, all these years later, they were still there.

Eden hated it. She would never be a northerner. She was shriveling up as a person and losing her identity completely. She was even prepared to admit that her mother and father had been right all along, and that she had been impulsive and immature. Eden wanted excitement, to meet interesting people, to go to plays and the beach. An independently wealthy businessman thrown into the fantasy wouldn't hurt either.

The ammunition was unnecessary.

Eden stepped backwards into the house and returned to the living room. Except for the dust and the dead houseplants, the living room was arranged the same way it had been three years earlier. A big, oversized chair sat near the bay window facing the drive, the sofa that Sophie slumbered on was angled toward the fireplace. There was a stand with the TV on the left side of it and a bookshelf on the right. A wedding photo of Eden and Cade was propped up on the mantle. She picked it up and blew off the dust.

She and Cade married five years ago, shortly after she'd discovered she was pregnant. They didn't have money for a big wedding and ended up tying the knot at a courthouse with a justice of the peace. She'd always dreamed about the fairytale wedding and thought they'd at least get married in a church. Her parents had flown in for the occasion and even though it was low-key, Eden had bought a white dress, and Cade had rented a tux. She studied his face in the photo. Dark hair framed attractive features. He had his arm possessively around his bride. Eden was smiling too widely, she thought, her auburn, eighties-big-hair curls sprayed into submission with copious amounts of hairspray. Her eyes were bluish, wide with wonder, and, she thought, ignorance. She flipped the photo onto its face.

"Sophie." Eden shook her daughter gently until she awoke. "Hey, sleepy head, wake up. We're at Grandma's house."

Sophie pulled herself into an upright position and pointed, "Is that Grandma, Mommy?"

Lorraine was watering the plants. Eden watched with dismay as her mother filled each pot to the very rim and then left to fill her jug again. No wonder all the plants were dead.

"Yes, yes it is."

Lorraine came back with another jug of water, and systematically abused the next two plants.

"Mom, I think that's enough water for now." Eden gently pulled the jug out of her mother's hand and led her over to the sofa. "This is Sophie. She was only a baby the last time you saw her."

"Hi, Grandma," Sophie said in a shy whisper.

"Hi, Eden. Is school out already?"

"I'm not Eden, I'm Sophie," Sophie said, twisting her face to show her indignation, but Lorraine was already on her way back to the kitchen.

"Are you hungry, sweetie pie?" Eden said, diverting her daughter's attention.

"Uh-hum."

"How 'bout pizza?" Eden offered, knowing there was nothing in the house to eat.

"Okay," Sophie said, her little voice insecure. Eden brushed back wisps of Sophie's blond hair, hooking it behind her ears.

"It's going to be okay, Sophie."

"When is Daddy coming?"

"We've talked about this already, sweetheart. You and I are going to live with Grandma for a little while, so don't worry yourself over it. I'm going to call the pizza man now. Why don't you watch cartoons, until it comes?"

Eden made the call from the only phone in the house, which, unlike her own cordless which she had forgotten in Landers, trapped her in the kitchen, making her feel like a dog on a leash.

Lorraine was circling the kitchen, opening all the cupboard doors and then closing them again. Eden decided to ignore her and filled the sink with hot sudsy water. She started in on the dishes and wiped down the table and counters. She was exhausted but she hated waking up to a dirty kitchen, and she planned to go straight to bed after they finished dinner.

She retrieved the broom from the closet and started sweeping. Lorraine approached her from behind. "What are you doing?" She snatched the broom away. "I know you think I can't take care of my own house, but I can clean it perfectly well."

"Okay." Eden raised her hands in surrender. "You can do the sweeping." She sat quietly agonizing as she watched her mother hopelessly move dirt around the kitchen floor. She rested her head in her hands, exhausted.

The day had started off badly enough and Cade hadn't made it easy. They'd stayed up most of the night before arguing. No, arguing wasn't the right word, she thought, since they hadn't been shouting. They were just tense. They never shouted, and maybe that was part of the problem. They *deliberated*. She'd replayed their conversation a million times on the trip down. She'd done the right thing, she was sure of it, but that didn't mean it felt good.

"Don't do this, Eden," Cade had said, his voice quiet and terse.

Eden pressed her fingertips into her forehead, trying to massage the headache that pounded there. "I should've done it long ago."

Cade was suddenly in front of her, grabbing her shoulders. "I don't want you to go." His dark eyes blazed with pain, and she broke his gaze. She didn't mean to hurt him. She just couldn't keep going on this way.

"I'm sorry," she mustered. "I'm leaving in the morning."

"With Sophie?" Eden couldn't miss the hitch in his voice.

"She needs me."

"She needs me, too, Eden." He released his hold and paced the room, raking both hands through his cropped hair. Then he turned back to her. "You always get what you want don't you?" he spewed. "You just do what you want no matter who gets hurt."

Those words stung. They'd hurt her vanity. Eden didn't like to think of herself as insensitive to the needs of others, but of course, Cade was just speaking out of anger.

"It was a mistake, Cade."

"What? Us?"

"Yes," she'd said softly.

Cade lowered his head, defeated. "It was never a mistake for me."

That morning he'd put on a pleasant face for Sophie's sake, giving her a long hug and a lot of kisses on her forehead, and making sure she was safely buckled into her car seat.

"You can change your mind, Eden."

She shook her head and jumped into the car. She never looked back.

~

The doorbell rang, shaking Eden from her reverie. She got up to answer it.

"Pizza here." The young man handed Eden the box and gave her a slip to sign. "Uh, the boss wanted me to tell you that the account needs to be paid up soon." He seemed embarrassed. "Uh, if it's not, he'll be closing the account. I mean, it's usually payment on delivery only, eh? But Joe made an exception for Mrs. Emerson for some reason."

"That's okay. I'll pay it now. What's the total?"

"Ninety-three, seventy-two."

Eden gulped. He had to be kidding. How much pizza did Mom eat? It was her turn to stammer. "Uh, uh, just a minute. I'll get my cheque book." She filled out the cheque and signed it, all the while wondering how many other such accounts her mother had open out there.

Eden dished out the pizza onto three plates and poured three glasses of water from the tap. No milk or juice in the fridge.

"Who was at the door?" Lorraine asked, "Was it Josh? Is he home yet?"

"No, Mom. It was the pizza guy."

Watching Lorraine eat made Eden feel nauseated. Lorraine swiped a length of greasy hair off her face, smearing her wrinkled skin with sauce. A pineapple chunk dropped onto her sweater.

"Is Josh home yet?"

"No," she replied wearily. "He's not."

Lorraine hadn't even swallowed before asking again, "Is Josh home, yet?"

Suddenly, Eden felt like screaming. She was physically and mentally spent from the split from Cade, the nine-hour drive, and now this. Why couldn't things just go her way for once? She stood sharply and cleaned up, putting the left over pizza in the fridge.

"Time for bed, Sophie. Mommy's really tired."

Chapter Three

1946

Lorrie trod softly around the sleeping figure to the open window. She pulled the glass panels closed, and slipped the lock. Even though a cool breeze had flushed out the room, the taint of sickness never lifted. It was part of the room as sure as the bed, dresser and chair were that occupied it.

All of Lorrie's memories of her mother were tied to this room. She once overheard her father tell a neighbour that Ma had never been the same since the baby. How she had caused her mother's illness, she never knew.

Laboured breath escaped through bluish, chapped lips. Lorrie tenderly applied ointment to soften them, rousing the sleeper awake.

"My dear, Lorrie."

"I didn't mean to wake you, Ma."

"That's fine. Heaven knows I sleep enough."

"Here, drink this." Lorrie lifted a glass of tepid water, and propped up her mother's head. The woman took three meager sips then let her head drop.

"The roses have died." Three soft stems were bent over, scattering dry petals on the floor.

"I'll bring you new ones, Ma."

"Not just yet. Sit down with me for a moment." Lorrie rested on the edge of the bed. "You take good care of me. I wish I could have been a better mother to you."

"Hush, Ma. You can't help…"

"I know. Now, listen to me." She reached for Lorrie's hand. "I'm thankful for the few times since you were born, when I was strong enough to sit in the living room, and even sometimes to work in my gardens. It makes my heart glad to see that you love them, too."

"If it weren't for me, you would be well!"

"Lorrie Williams! You mustn't think like that. You are the best thing that ever happened to me. A gift from God himself!" She paused, breathing in short breaths. "You've made many sacrifices to make me happy. Don't think I don't know it. I want you to be happy now. Soon…"

"Ma, please, don't."

"Yes. When it's time, don't grieve long for me. Take your life and live it to the fullest."

"Ma, someday you will be well." She patted her mother's thin, bony hand with feigned confidence. "Now, I need to get supper ready. You just rest. I'll come back to check on you shortly."

Lorrie stood up to leave. Pa would be home from the mill soon, and he expected something hot on the table.

About the Author

Lee Strauss is the author of The Minstrel Series (contemporary romance), The Perception Series (young adult dystopian) and young adult historical fiction. She is the married mother of four grown children, three boys and a girl, and divides her time between British Columbia, Canada and Dresden, Germany. When she's not writing or reading she likes to cycle, hike and do yoga. She enjoys traveling (but not jet lag :0), soy lattes, red wine and dark chocolate.

She also writes younger YA fantasy as Elle Strauss.

SONG LINKS

The Christmas Song (remake) by Bethany Petch
The Christmas Song by Andrew Smith

Listen to all the songs from The Minstrel Series on Bandcamp at songsfromtheminstrel.bandcamp.com

Scan the QR code to hear the songs featured in
Peace & Goodwill

Want more info and features about The Minstrel Series?
Visit TheMinstrelSeries.blogspot.com.

ARTIST LINKS

Andrew Smith

andrewsmithmusic.com

Bethany Petch

facebook.com/BethanyPetch

ACKNOWLEDGEMENTS

A big shout out goes to my fabulous beta readers, A.M. Offenwanger, Denise Jaden and Juanita Rose; my editor Marie Jaskulka, cover designer, Steven Novak, and formatter Ali Cross, who all play a very important role in getting my books out! A special shout out to Debbie Moore for her British authenticity notes!

Thank you to Andrew Smith for writing an amazing song and to Bethany Petch for her tremendous vocal interpretation.

I would be lost without the on-line writing community. I'm so grateful for each and every friend I've made, even though I haven't met most of them in real life. Kudos to my street team for cheering my on and helping me to spread the word!

Thanks to Hans Christian Anderson for writing The Little Matchstick Girl.

As always I'm forever grateful to my husband, Norm Strauss who not only offers me an abundance of moral support but produces the music that goes with this series, to my kids for making my life a joy, and to my friends who keep me grounded, especially Marie Clarke, Lori Van Zyderveld and the "noble girls" - Donna Petch, Shawn Giesbrecht and Norine Stewart for your enthusiasm, prayer and laughs.

BOOKS BY LEE STRAUSS

Contemporary Romance
East of the Sun

The Minstrel Series
Sun & Moon
Flesh & Bone
Heart & Soul
Peace & Goodwill (~ a Christmas novella)

Sci-fi Mystery Romance
A Nursery Rhyme Suspense
Run Run Run (The Gingerbread Man Episode 1/Part 1)

Young Adult/Dystopian
The Perception Trilogy
Ambition (short story prequel)
Perception (book 1)
Volition (book 2)
Contrition (book 3)

Historical Fiction
Jars of Clay (vol. 1)
Broken Vessels (vol. 2)

Playing with Matches

For news of new releases and promotions,
sign up for Lee's newsletter at: **leestraussbooks.com**

Made in the USA
Charleston, SC
15 November 2014